High

Even in
**Another
World!**

5

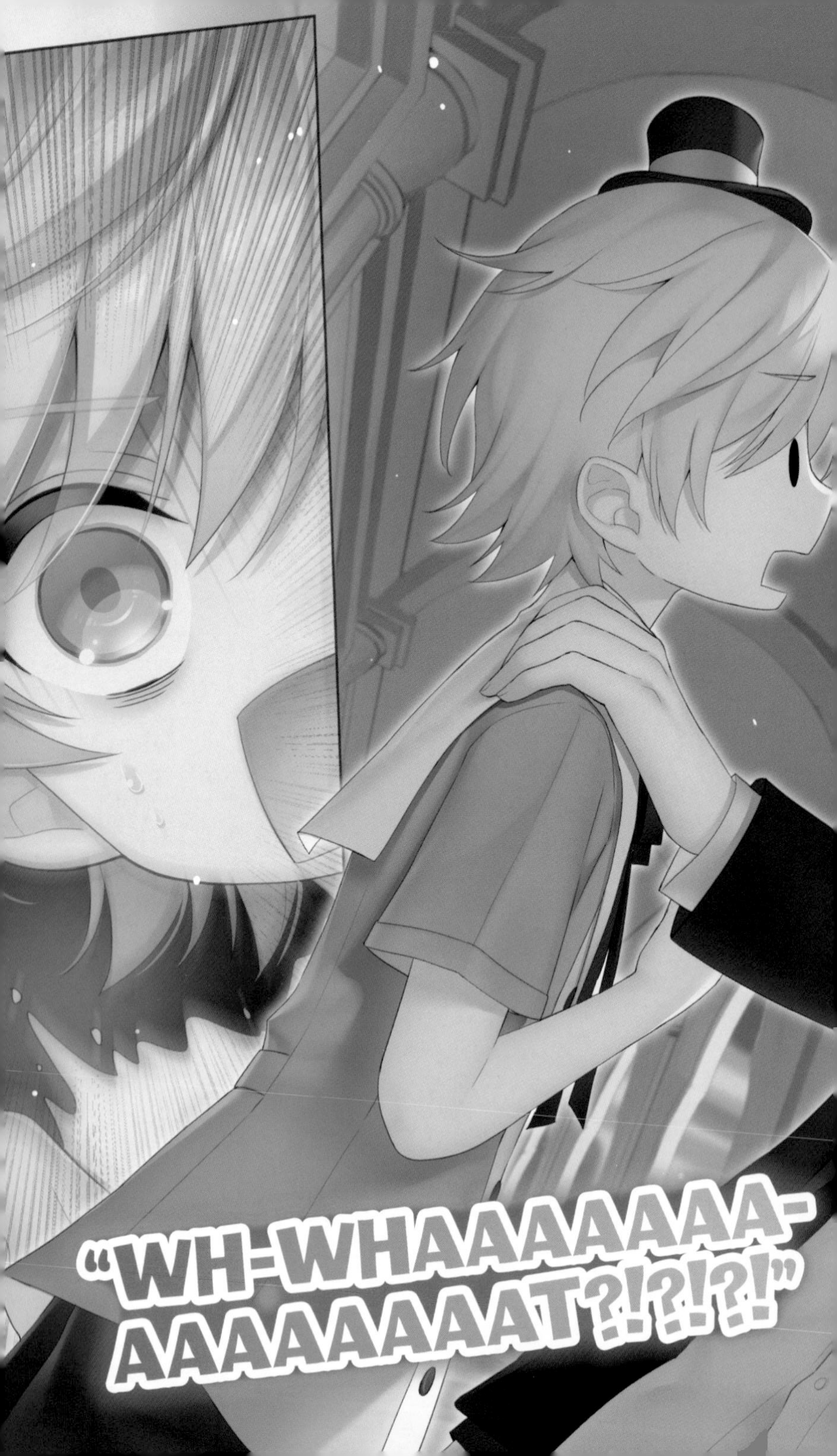
"WH-WHAAAAAAAA-
AAAAAAAAAT?!?!?!"

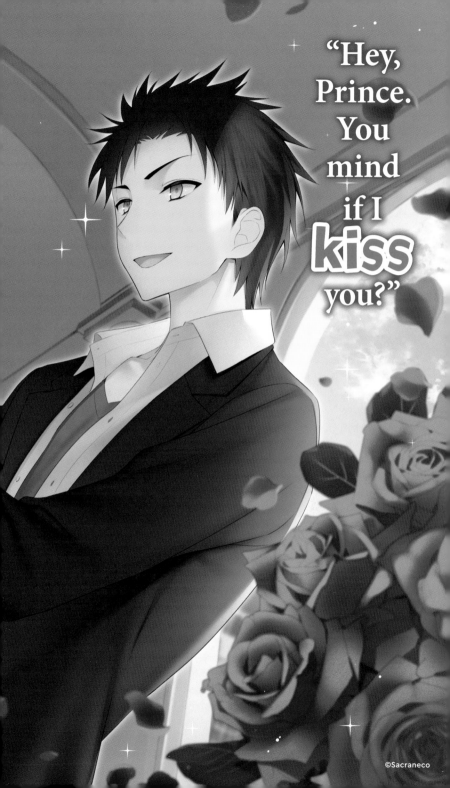

"Hey, Prince. You mind if I **kiss** you?"

©Sacraneco

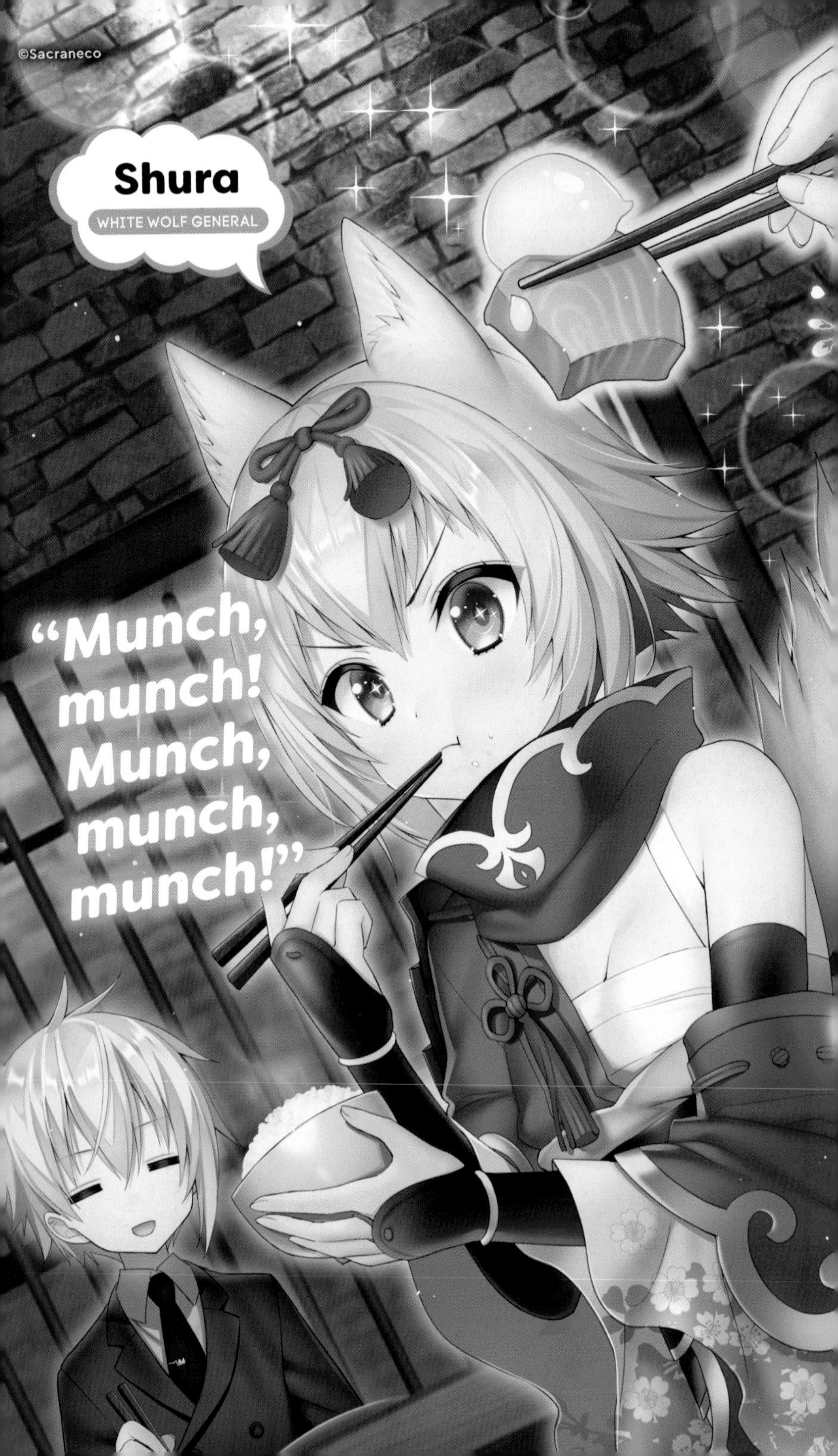

©Sacraneco
Shura
WHITE WOLF GENERAL
"Munch, munch! Munch, munch, munch!"

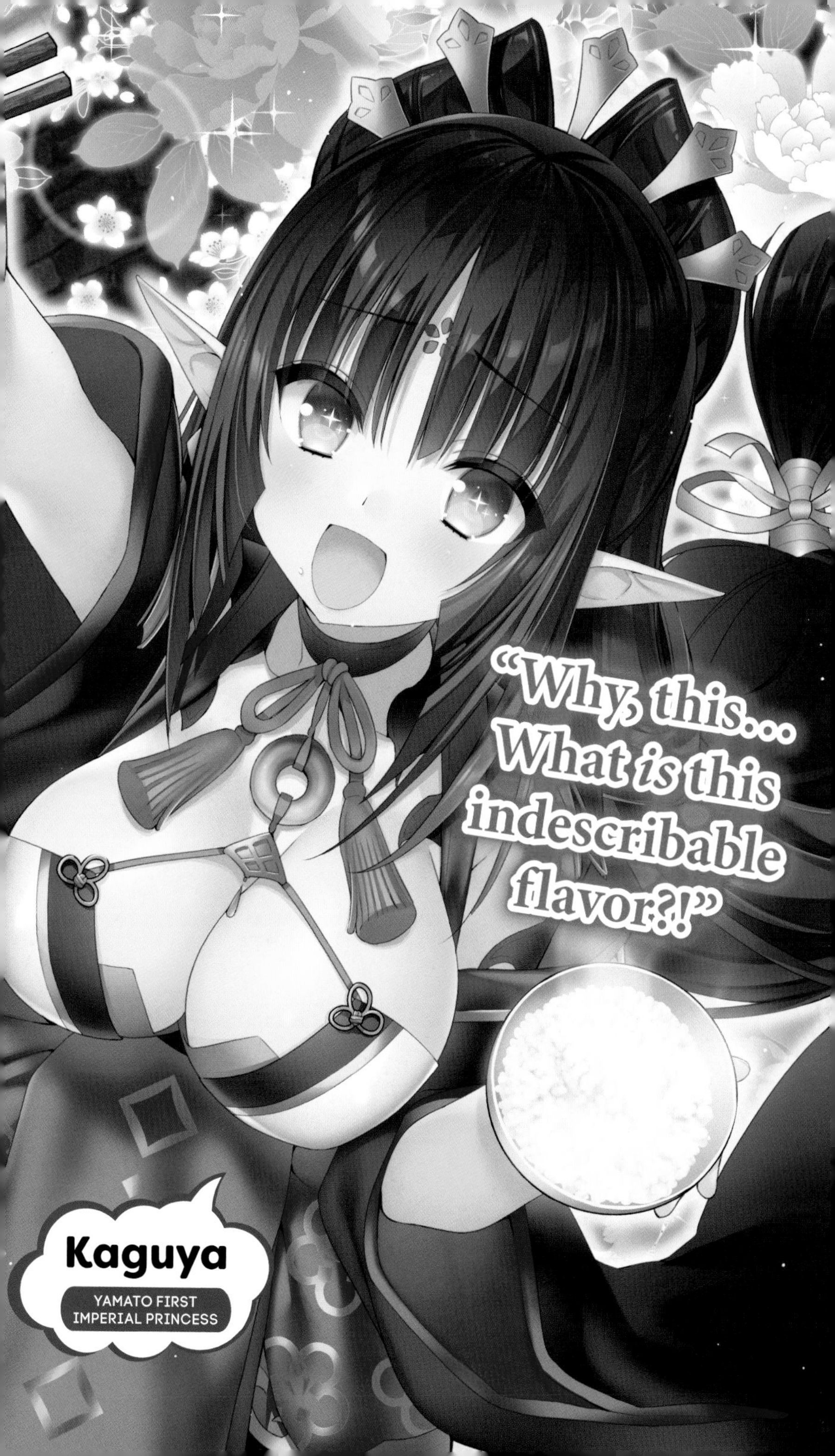
"Why, this... What *is* this indescribable flavor?!"
Kaguya
YAMATO FIRST IMPERIAL PRINCESS

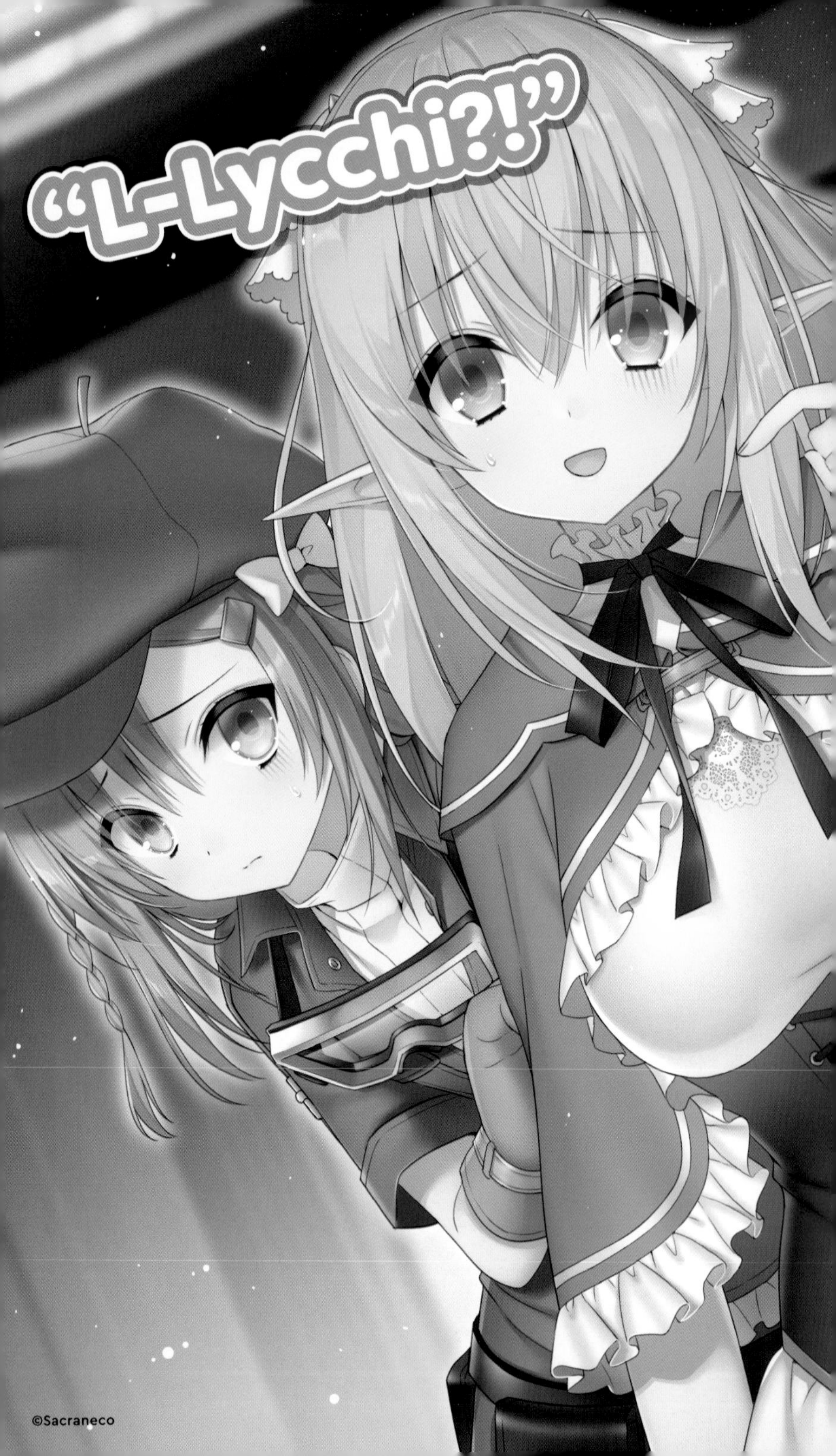
"L-Lycchi?!"
©Sacraneco

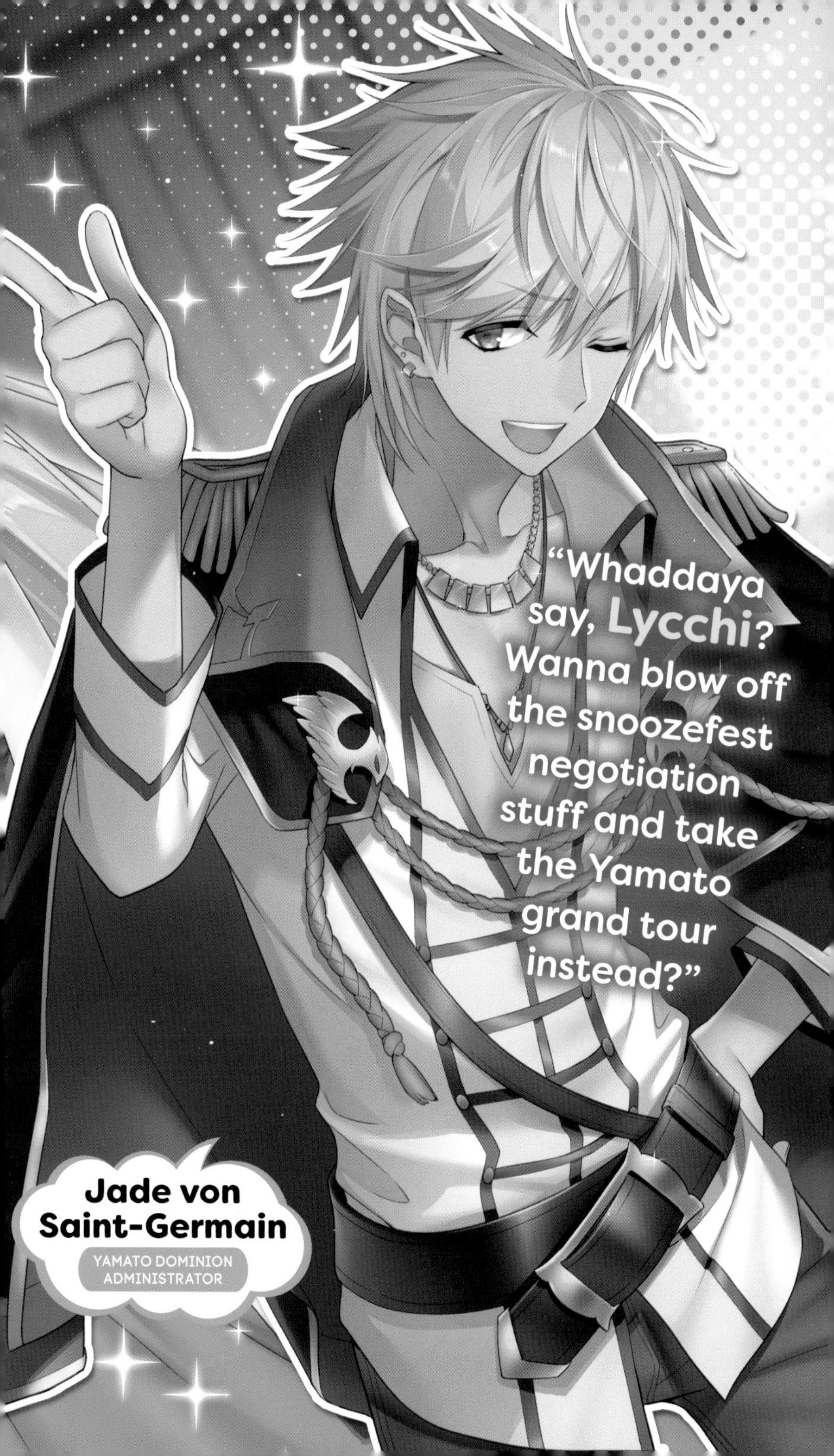
"Whaddaya say, Lycchi? Wanna blow off the snoozefest negotiation stuff and take the Yamato grand tour instead?"
Jade von Saint-Germain
YAMATO DOMINION ADMINISTRATOR

CONTENTS

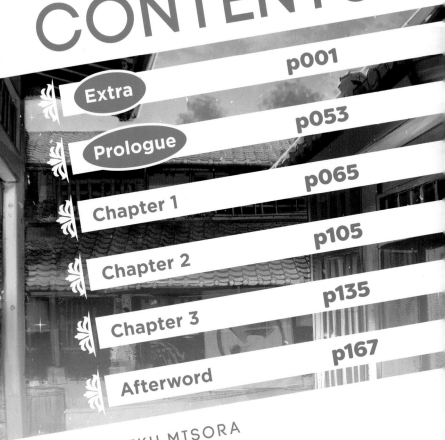

RIKU MISORA
ILLUSTRATION BY
SACRANECO

High School Prodigies
Have It Easy Even in
Another World!

High School Prodigies Have It Easy Even in Another World!

5

Riku Misora

Illustration by SACRANECO

YEN ON
NEW YORK

High School Prodigies Have It EaSy Even in Another World! 5

Riku Misora

TRANSLATION BY NATHANIEL HIROSHI THRASHER
COVER ART BY SACRANECO

CHOUJIN KOUKOUSEI TACHI WA ISEKAI DEMO YOYU DE IKINUKU YOUDESU! vol. 5
Copyright © 2017 Riku Misora
Illustrations copyright © 2017 Sacraneco
First published in Japan in 2017 by SB Creative, Tokyo.
English translation rights arranged with SB Creative, Tokyo through Tuttle-Mori Agency, Inc., Tokyo.

English translation © 2021 by Yen Press, LLC

Yen On
150 West 30th Street, 19th Floor
New York, NY 10001

Visit us at yenpress.com
facebook.com/yenpress ★ twitter.com/yenpress
yenpress.tumblr.com ★ instagram.com/yenpress

First Yen On Edition: October 2021

Yen On is an imprint of Yen Press, LLC.
The Yen On name and logo are trademarks of Yen Press, LLC.

The publisher is not responsible for websites (or their content) that
are not owned by the publisher.

Library of Congress Cataloging-in-Publication Data
Names: Misora, Riku, author. | Sacraneco, illustrator. | Thrasher, Nathaniel Hiroshi, translator.
Title: High school prodigies have it easy even in another world! / Riku Misora ;
illustration by Sacraneco ; translation by Nathaniel Hiroshi Thrasher.
Other titles: Chōjin-Kokoseitachi wa Isekai demo Yoyu de Ikinuku Yōdesu! English
Identifiers: LCCN 2020016894 | ISBN 9781975309725 (v. 1 ; trade paperback) |
ISBN 9781975309749 (v. 2 ; trade paperback) | ISBN 9781975309763 (v.3 ; trade paperback) |
ISBN 9781975309787 (v. 4 ; trade paperback) | ISBN 9781975309800 (v. 5 ; trade paperback) |
Subjects: CYAC: Fantasy. | Gifted persons—Fiction. | Imaginary places—Fiction | Magic—Fiction.
Classification: LCC PZ7.M6843377 Hi 2020 | DDC [Fic]—dc23
LC record available at https://lccn.loc.gov/2020016894

ISBNs: 978-1-9753-0980-0 (paperback)
978-1-9753-0981-7 (ebook)

1 3 5 7 9 10 8 6 4 2

LSC-C

Printed in the United States of America

The (Self-Proclaimed) Genius from the Empire

Shortly after the armistice with the empire was signed, the High School Prodigies were busy getting ready for the currency issuance and the national elections.

Over in the Buchwald province, a merchant caravan heading toward the empire was attacked by a group of highwaymen.

When the region's former lord and current provisional governor, Buchwald, heard what had happened, he immediately assembled a unit to deal with the outlaws and dispatched his force to the old fortress that the thieves were using as a hideout.

"There it is, right up ahead."

At the end of the forest path, the Order of the Seven Luminaries' members tasked with handling the bandits reached a gently sloping hill. Atop it sat an ancient stone garrison.

The structure was erected by a nation that fell long before the empire first claimed the territory.

"Thanks to the Seven Luminaries, people have it better than ever. You'd have to be a real scumbag to turn to banditry these days."

"Maybe they're nobles who're afraid of getting purged?"

"Y'know, that might be it. I heard a couple of 'em tried something like that over in Gustav."

"Cut the chatter. The merchants said the robbers had guns. We're almost in firing range, and there's no cover out here. Make sure to keep your shields at the ready."

"Ha. I dunno what kinda weapons those guys have, but these babies from the Seven Luminaries will make 'em look like peashooters."

"Yeah. The minute they stick their heads up, we'll blow 'em full of holes."

As they spoke, the fifty-odd soldiers sent to subdue the criminals readied their weapons. Each was equipped with one of the Seven Luminaries' mass-produced bolt-action rifles.

The guns boasted unprecedented firing rates and ballistic stability because gunpowder was packed into the bullets themselves.

In a world where matchlock firearms were still commonplace, these armaments stood head and shoulders above the general level of technology.

Once, this group of men sent to quell the thieves had been a part of the imperial forces. The sheer difference in power between their current equipment and the matchlock guns they were accustomed to had them feeling giddy.

Their captain could hardly blame them, though.

Ultimately, bandits were nothing more than rowdy amateurs. They didn't stand a chance against a trained military incursion.

Between that and the Seven Luminaries' advanced weaponry, this was no battle the dispatched contingent was walking into. It was a hunt, and all they were doing was rounding up a few mangy strays. This simple errand would take no more than a few quick minutes.

As such, the captain thought there was no need to get worked up about it. Quickly ending things was best. However, a cry from somewhere above interrupted the captain's thoughts.

"Hey, whoa! Slow down there, little rats! The hell you think you're doing, skittering around someone's house like that?!" cried a husky, grating voice that rolled down from somewhere atop the hill.

The captain squinted.

Roughly three hundred feet ahead were three people standing on top of the fortress's ramparts.

It was the thieves.

The one shouting was a tall, lanky man leaning out over the wall with his foot perched atop it. His appearance gave off the impression of a lean, ragged wolf. By the looks of it, he was the group's leader.

Having now received visual confirmation of their targets, the captain retrieved the Republic of Elm banner from one of his men and held it aloft as he shouted back, "We, the Order of the Seven Luminaries, serve the exalted God Akatsuki! I take it you're the bandits who've been terrorizing the merchants in this area as of late!"

"And so what if we are?!"

"The Elm Provisional Government has a warrant out for your arrest! Throw down your weapons and surrender peacefully! If you resist, we won't hesitate to shoot you down where you stand, and we'll barely have to lift a finger to do so! Now, make your choice! Will you submit to the law, or would you rather die crawling on the ground like dogs?!"

A few warning shots rang out from among the assembled soldiers, as if to emphasize the captain's ultimatum.

Entirely unperturbed, the bandit leader responded by laughing so hard his body shook.

"Ha-ha-ha! You hear that, boys?! They're here to *arrest* us! What a joke! You bastards stole a whole damn country from Freyjagard, so what makes you any better than us?!"

"How dare you! That affront against the angels won't stand!" the captain shouted back, indignant.

"Don't go tryin' to act tough on us. While you cowards were off double-crossing the empire, we've been out here surviving by ourselves. Now, why don't you turn tail and run before we hafta tear you chumps a couple new puckered-up assholes!"

The man's vulgar taunt earned a chorus of crude guffaws from his comrades.

"Lowlife scum…!"

The soldiers' orders were to capture them alive "if possible."

There was no need to offer the ruffians any further clemency.

And so the captain made his decision. "If you're that determined to die a dog's death, then we'll happily oblige you!"

"Oh, someone's gonna be dying, all right!"

Not a moment later, two holes formed in the front and the back of the captain's head. Gray matter gushed out.

"_____"

"What?!"

His body slumped ungracefully onto the grass.

The troops were unable to make sense of their commanding officer's sudden death.

""""Eat shit!!!!"""""

""""Aaaaaaaaaargh!!!!"""""

Unfortunately, hardly a moment later, the front line of soldiers got mowed down by a hail of bullets from atop the ramparts.

Shot after shot rang out, and the fresh spring grass was stained with vivid splashes of red.

The soldiers panicked. As former imperial troops, they knew the capabilities of their world's standard firearms.

Matchlock guns had an effective firing range of one hundred fifty feet. Striking a target in the head while they were three hundred feet away shouldn't have been possible.

Even so, the deadly projectiles were claiming the soldiers' lives in rapid succession. Their enemies had gotten the drop on them from a distance that far exceeded their expectations.

Just before the Seven Luminaries' force broke formation and fled, their vice captain called out from the rearguard. "Shields up and out! Anybody who has one, gather at the front and form a wall!"

""""Yes sir!""""

As his voice cut crisply through the chaos, all the soldiers equipped with duralumin shields rushed to the front of the group to protect their allies.

However, the source of their confusion remained.

"Dammit, what the hell's going on?! We shouldn't be in matchlock range yet!"

The soldiers winced as bullets pummeled their shields.

Despite being the one who gave the order, the vice captain was just as perplexed as his charges. The enemy was raining lead on them with ease from over one hundred fifty feet away. He'd never heard of guns that could do that—*except the Seven Luminaries'.*

What's more, the shots were coming without so much as a pause or break between them.

This doesn't make any sense... The vice commander bit his lip in consternation.

"Ha-ha-ha! What's wrong, dickheads?! We ain't even done with the foreplay yet and you're already losin' steam! After all that big talk, you're just gonna huddle up like little turtles?!"

The bandits' crude laughter echoed down from the hill as discord and confusion ate away at the gathered troops.

While crass, the thieves had a point. Huddling up like that was only making the soldiers easier targets.

The vice captain issued his next set of orders. "Dammit... All right, maintain defensive formation and advance! Our guns may be better, but they have the advantage as long as they're holed up in that fortress!"

""""Yes sir!"""""

Those outfitted with shields did as instructed, working together to block attacks from both the front and overhead, safeguarding the riflemen behind them as the force slowly began making its way forward.

It was at times like these that their rigorous training was evident, for their defense was impeccable. Every last one of the bullets raining down on them bounced off their duralumin barriers.

All they had to do was march slowly toward the fortress, then blow its gate open with grenades. From there, they could storm the building and gain control from within. Yet right as the vice captain's heart began to swell—

"Ha-ha! Didn't anyone ever tell you there's no point tryin' to come inside if you're gonna use that much protection?! Hey, boys, let's give these limp dicks something to perk 'em up!"

""""Whooooooo-hooooooo!"""""

—a deafening roar shook the air.

Every soldier on that hill recognized that sound, for they had heard it before countless times. It was like a gunshot, only hundreds of times deeper. There was no mistaking it.

Artillery fire...?!

""""AAAAAAAAAAGH!!!!"""""

The effect was immediate. In the blink of an eye, a full half of the company got blown to smithereens. The explosion sent scraps of shredded flesh flying through the air. It had come from a device sticking out over the rampart walls.

"They have a mortar!"

"How did a bunch of crooks get their hands on something like that?!"

None of the troops had ever heard of bandits using a mortar. What would thieves ever need with such a thing? It would blow up all the money they were after. If they were equipped with such a powerful weapon, it could only mean one thing.

These are no ordinary criminals! the vice captain realized.

After narrowly avoiding the mortar fire, he shouted an order to the other survivors. "Everyone, retreat! We're falling back to the spriiiiiiing!!"

Their will to fight broken, the soldiers turned heel and fled as fast as they could.

"Ha-ha-ha! Ah-ha-ha-ha-ha!!!!"

The bandits jeered and mocked as they watched the routed soldiers beat their retreat.

"Why, if it isn't an angel!"

"And Mr. Buchwald, to boot. What brings you two over to our oily little corner of the world?"

"Just a little business to attend to with Ringo."

After the Order of the Seven Luminaries' contingent was routed by the heavily armed bandits, former marquis Buchwald immediately sent word to the leader of Elm's provisional government, Tsukasa Mikogami.

When Tsukasa heard the news, he turned to Ringo Oohoshi to gain a better understanding of the situation. At present, Ringo was in the new workshop she had built in Dulleskoff to analyze a certain something.

Tsukasa and Buchwald waited in the workshop's break room for her to finish working.

After they shot the breeze with the workshop staff for a while, Ringo and her robot assistant, Bearabbit, appeared.

"Sorry...for the wait! And sorry...it took so long..."

"Not at all. If anything, I should be apologizing to you for interrupting while you're so busy. So...what did you find when you inspected the bullets retrieved from our soldiers' bodies?"

"S-sure enough...there were rifling marks."

"So they *do* have rifles," Tsukasa murmured. "I had my suspicions when I heard about the range they were firing from, but now we know for certain."

Buchwald cut in. "Wh-when you say 'rifles,' you're referring to the guns you Seven Luminaries produce with the, um, spirals inside the barrels, right? But then...how did a bunch of thieves get their hands on our guns?"

"That's not...it...," Ringo said, refuting Buchwald's point. However, noticing Ringo's poor oratory skills and general shyness, Bearabbit stepped in to elaborate on her behalf.

"The bullets we use in our rifles all have the exact same koalaties, but the lead balls we removed from our soldiers were the kind this world was using befur us."

Buchwald's eyes went wide. "N-now that you mention it, I remember Mr. Archride saying something about that back when we visited your arms factory—about how the imperial workshops had a gun with spiral grooves that could strike accurately even at long distances."

Tsukasa nodded. "That's right; we weren't the first in this world to develop rifling. However, the empire shelved development on the technology due to cost issues and the fact that they wanted to prioritize upgrading their army from matchlock to flintlock guns instead. I imagine what the bandits had were imperial prototypes of some sort."

"B-but shelved development or not, could a bunch of common bandits really get their hands on things like a mortar and weapons with cutting-edge imperial technology?"

"..."

Buchwald's question made Tsukasa go silent.

As far as the young prime minister knew, those ruffians should never have been able to so much as glimpse such things. The imperial workshops were no less than the beating heart of the Freyjagard Empire's military. Their prototypes weren't the sort of thing common fugitives could just casually acquire. And more importantly…

The rifles aside, what do a bunch of mountain bandits need with a mortar?

Folks like them favored armaments designed for robbery, not destruction. It was hard to imagine them shelling out the kind of money a mortar would cost for a weapon that was liable to destroy the very things they were trying to steal.

Still, just because it was unlikely didn't mean it was outright impossible. There were undoubtedly times when military surplus made its way into bandits' hands. They might have merely acquired the mortar on a whim. It was certainly possible.

However, there's also no shortage of nobles who don't exactly hold Grandmaster Neuro's peace treaty in high regard.

Knowing this, it was hard for Tsukasa to deny the possibility that this could be the work of an influential imperial noble arming the outlaws in the hope of causing discord between Elm and Freyjagard.

Tsukasa's instincts as a prodigious politician told him that such a possibility was the clear frontrunner. If it was true, though, then it made things messy.

At the moment, the Republic of Elm was in the middle of a nationwide campaign to improve relations with the empire.

Even if this is the work of an imperial aristocrat, given the damage it would do to our relationship, I would just as soon avoid exposing that fact.

Was that dishonest? Perhaps. But the blind pursuit of the truth wasn't what politics was all about.

No matter who the bandits had backing them, it was in Elm's best interests to deal with the situation as if it were an isolated event. To that end, Tsukasa chose to dodge Buchwald's question—

"Let's set aside the issue of how the bandits sourced their weapons for the moment. We won't know that for sure until we round them up and hear it from the horse's mouth, after all. What we need to focus on is neutralizing them."

—and instead turned the conversation to their immediate future.

"Under normal circumstances, I would prefer having the people of this world deal with the problem on their own, but the situation is a little too hairy for that. Not only did the robbers get their hands on some serious firepower, but they're also holding an easily defensible position. Having the people of this world try to take it would cost a lot of lives. That's where you come in, Bearabbit."

"*Fur what?*"

"After Aoi, you're the strongest combatant we have. I want you to clear the fortress. I recognize that it's an overreach on our part, but this incident has already claimed more than its fair share of lives. I want to end things without any more casualties. Can I count on you?"

Bearabbit had no reason to turn down Tsukasa's request. He was all too happy to help.

"*Of course! It'll bearly take me a—*"

Yet the moment he tried to take on the task—

"HOLD IT RIGHT THEEEEEEEERE!!!!"

—a youthful, high-pitched soprano rocked every pair of ears in the break room.

When they turned to see who the earsplitting shout had come from, they discovered a short girl striking an imposing stance at the entrance to the break room. She gave Tsukasa a willful stare.

"I couldn't help but overhear you, angel! And I must say, it vexes me you would write us off before even giving us a chance to prove ourselves! If all you need is a weapon that can mop fifty, even a hundred bandits, then while I can't speak for the humdrum masses, a GENIUS like me can make you one, no problem!"

As she spoke, the girl puffed up her tiny chest. She was a bit younger than Tsukasa and the other Prodigies.

All the other people who worked for Ringo were older than twenty, making this girl the most juvenile by far. She had platinum-blond hair rolled up into curly drills, and a black ribbon sat atop her head.

"You're one of the exchange students from the empire, aren't you?" Tsukasa asked, recalling who the girl was.

"That's me—Cranberry Diva, third daughter of Count Diva!"

The exchange student system was one of the methods that the Republic of Elm used to normalize relations between Elm and Freyjagard. The girl before them was one such scholar, there to learn about Elm's advanced engineering techniques.

"Mr. Angel! I ask that you leave this situation to me, the BIG GENIUS widely rumored to be next in line to head up the imperial workshops! I was just hoping to get a chance to show off the knowledge and skills I've obtained in your fine country, so I don't mind in the slightest!"

"Well, I did say I wished to have the people of this world deal with the problem on their own…"

Cranberry hyperventilated with excitement as she pressed forward, and Tsukasa found himself forced to recede a little as he spoke.

"C-Cranberry, that's enough! Don't go sticking your nose in where

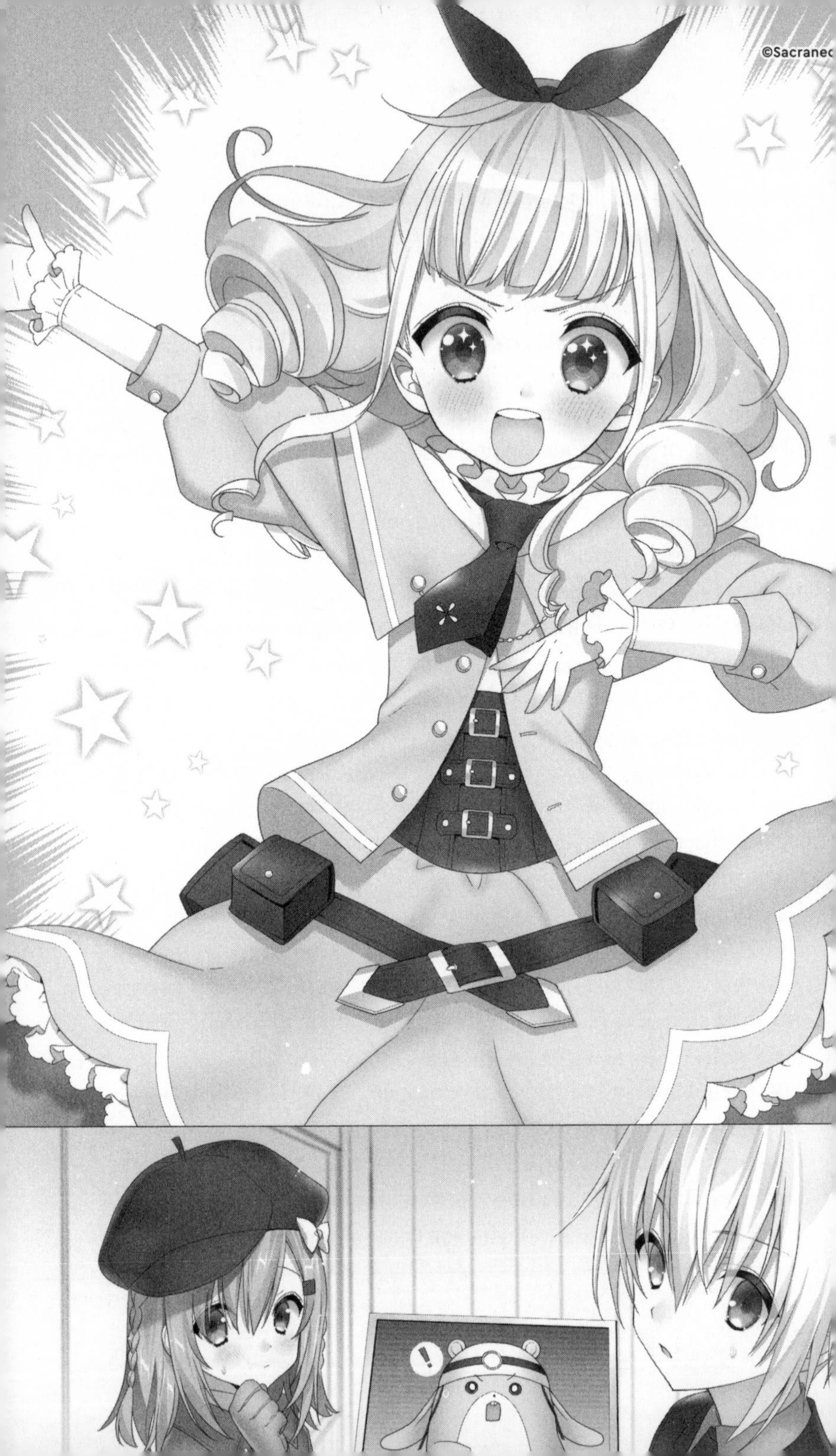
©Sacranec

it doesn't belong! If we just leave this to the angels, we get it all over with safely!" Buchwald chided. He had some familial relations with the Diva family. However, even his remonstrations weren't enough to get Cranberry to back down.

"Boo! Don't you believe in me, Unc? I am a GENIUS, remember. And I'll have you know that there isn't a machine in this workshop I haven't mastered!"

Tsukasa found himself impressed by both her ego and her initiative. He quietly posed a question to her teacher, Bearabbit. "…Bearabbit, what's your honest take on her abilities?"

"All the stuff about being the imperial workshops' next head is pawsitively made-up. But she indeed learned how to use all the machines and tools here on her beary furst day. By her third, she dismantled one of the machine tools and put it back together just fine during her spare time. I had to put a paws on it when she tried to do the same to one of the steam engines, but when I made it up to her by showing her its blueprint and explaining the principles and mechanisms behind it, she got her bearings in no time. As fur as motivation and tailent go, she's got everyone else in the workshop beat by a country mile."

"You don't say…," Tsukasa muttered. Bearabbit seemed to hold a high opinion of Cranberry.

Tsukasa could say the same of his own student, Nio Harvey. The way the exchange students had come to a country that their nation had been at war with just a few weeks prior to absorb their knowledge and skills betrayed a level of scholarly passion that was nothing short of admirable.

Compared to the people of Elm, their zeal was on a whole different level.

…I suppose we're primarily to blame for that.

Although doing so had been necessary to make up the difference in power between Elm and the empire, the Prodigies had given the people of Elm *a little too much*. It had robbed the denizens of their fervor. Tsukasa believed that had played a role in the failure to subjugate the bandits as well.

While it was true that the empire's rifles put more primitive weapons to shame, even they were little more than toys compared to the Order of the Seven Luminaries' bolt-action ones.

The Order's defeat could certainly be attributed to the fact that they were caught off-guard by their enemies' unforeseen firepower. Yet suppose they had just played things by the book and sent scouts out ahead to investigate their foes' capabilities beforehand. In that case, their equipment should still have given them an insurmountable edge.

They lost because they were careless.

Blinded by hubris at the hitherto-unseen weaponry at their disposal, the soldiers had cut corners and skipped critical steps. It was an unacceptable blunder.

Tsukasa knew that the best way to avoid repeating that failure would be to offer the people as little help as possible.

What's more, she's from the empire.

Tsukasa pictured the way things would unfold.

If it turned out that an imperial noble really was supplying weapons to the bandits, then the Elm government would have no choice but to demand they be prosecuted, as anything less would be challenging to justify to the people of Elm. However, doing so would invariably cause damage to the tenuously amicable relationship between the two nations. That would be playing right into their enemy's hands.

If another imperial aristocrat like Cranberry were the one to handle the situation, though, then that would muddy the waters considerably, giving Tsukasa a chance to settle the whole matter quietly. That was the best outcome he could hope for.

Covering up inconvenient truths was part of a politician's job, too. Tsukasa's choice was clear.

"Very well, Cranberry Diva. I leave the project in your hands."

"Really?!" The girl lit up with excitement.

Tsukasa nodded. "Who knows what the thieves will do if we try to starve them out. If this new weapon of yours can deal catastrophic damage to their fortress in a single blow, it will doubtlessly send them into a panic. From there, we'll be able to use that panic to storm the building before they know what hit them and thereby minimize our casualties. I want you to turn your intellect toward devising a method that will bring us to that outcome."

"Hmm-hmm! With my brains, it's a DONE DEAL!" Cranberry thumped her slim chest and exhaled excitedly through her nose.

"Now, if that's all decided, I have a meeting to hold! Come along now, HUMDRUM MASSES! I will allow you to assist in my grand design!"

At some point, workers had assembled to see what all the fuss was about, and Cranberry loudly took charge of them as she strode out of the break room.

As the adult workers watched the child who seemed almost too small to contain her impudence go—

"Ha-ha! Glad to see you're in high spirits as usual, young Cranberry!"

"Whatever you need, we're happy to help!"

—they called after her with cheers of adulation.

Watching them, Tsukasa voiced an entirely reasonable statement.

"Given the way she acts, I'm surprised none of you find her annoying."

The workers replied readily.

"Yeah, well, she pissed us off a bit at first, but…"

"After a while, we sorta got used to it."

"Honestly, it's kinda cute getting talked down to by a little girl."

"To tell you the truth, I want her to step on me with those tiny feet of hers…"

"Interesting. It seems there's an outbreak of degeneracy going around," Tsukasa remarked.

He thought it best not to stick around for too long.

After seeing the workers off, Tsukasa turned his attention to another matter.

"…Say, Ringo?"

"Hmm?"

"Not to say I don't trust her, but there are lives at stake here. If it becomes necessary, can I count on you to lend her a hand?"

"Yeah. Leave it…to me."

Ringo clenched her tiny hand into a fist as she gave her assent. Then, she and Bearabbit hurried along after Cranberry.

"Let me start by laying the situation bear."

After parting ways with Tsukasa and Buchwald, Ringo and her robot companion headed to the workshop's conference room and shut the blinds. Once the chamber was dark, Bearabbit booted up one of his functions as he spoke.

Pale light streamed out of his primary display and projected an image onto the floor.

"Whoa, what's that?!"

"This is what the furtress the bandits are bearicaded up in looks like from above—courtesy of God Akatsuki's bearvoyance!"

The truth was that the image had been taken by satellite, but it benefitted the Seven Luminaries more to explain it as being part of Akatsuki's divine power.

"God Akatsuki never fails to astound…"

"Praise be!"

"………"

Although the Prodigies weren't deceiving people out of malice, Ringo still felt a little guilty as she saw the workers believe Bearabbit's lie and gaze reverently at the image. She turned to look at it herself.

The picture projected on the floor started out as a flat overhead view of the fortress, but it soon began to rise thanks to Bearabbit's processing powers. By including data gleaned through visual analysis of the building and surrounding topography, he displayed the area in three dimensions.

"Whoa! That's wild!"

"*This is a model of the stronghold we need to capture. It was built on top of a small hill, and it's fortified by ramparts on all sides. With the Order of the Seven Luminbearies' current equipment, defeating the bandits bearicaded inside would assuredly cost us lives. But if we had some way to take down the furtress's beariers to bruin the bandits' advantage, we could keep our sacrifices to a minimum. We want you all to pool your imaginations together and create a tool—a weapon—that can make that pawsible.*"

The workers reacted to this request with consternation.

"W-wait, us…? That's a pretty tough ask…"

"It's taking all we have just to make the *regular* guns, let alone come up with something new."

While Ringo stood among their timid ranks, she started thinking about what kind of tool would let them take the fortress without losing any soldiers.

The first thing that came to mind was a long-range missile strike.

With that, they'd be able to take down the castle from a safe distance.

Unfortunately, she was the only one present with the facilities and modern engineering knowledge required to pull that off.

To prevent that world from descending into a needless arms race, the Prodigies had decided not to publicize the manufacturing methods for TNT or other military-grade explosives. Instead, they passed them off as divine blessings. Most of the world was stuck with ordinary gunpowder. Presently, the only way to get huge amounts of firepower was to use similarly vast quantities of gunpowder.

The goal was to break the bandits' will to fight in a single blow, so whatever the workers used needed to be at least strong enough to blow one of the bastion's four walls to smithereens.

Such a task demanded ten full barrels of gunpowder, if not more.

Missiles did exist in this world, as Lakan had invented a gunpowder-packed "fire rocket." Yet, despite their intimidating looks, their destructive and propulsive capabilities were both middling at best, so all they were really used for was psychological warfare. Getting such projectiles to ferry the payload necessary to destroy a fortified rampart was out of the question.

Imperial mages did have a technique where they strengthened gunpowder into "purified gunpowder," which slightly amplified the thrust and power it generated. However, at the end of the day, it wasn't much better. It couldn't hold a candle to military-grade high explosives.

That sort of method just wasn't going to be realistic.

They would need to look somewhere else.

"Hey, I got an idea! What if we just made a giant-ass cannon and blew the fort to kingdom come?!" The young *byuma* who'd voiced the suggestion spread his arms out wide. Sure enough, building a giant cannon to bomb the bastion was the next logical step.

Sadly—

"Nah, there's no way. We don't have the raw materials here to fabricate something like that."

"Plus, it'd be way too expensive. We're workin' on a budget here, man."

"And even if we built it, how're we supposed to get it over there? The fortress ain't exactly close by."

—just as the others pointed out, that wasn't a practical solution, either.

Earth actually had a monstrous cannon like that named Mons Meg. At thirteen feet long and twenty inches in diameter, the nearly seven-ton weapon was nothing short of a behemoth. Just as the workers had pointed out, it came with a laundry list of defects. Its weight made it unwieldy to move, it was difficult to aim, its accuracy was horrendous, and on top of all that, the massive amounts of gunpowder it used made its barrel so hot that it needed hours to cool down before it could be reloaded.

Even its awe-inspiring form served as a mark against it as well. If, by some miracle, the cannon struck its target the first time, the enemy would have fled by the time it was ready to be used again.

Constructing a massive cannon here would only be a repeat of Mons Meg's sordid history on Earth.

Once the bandits fled, there would be nothing stopping them from preying on innocent people once more. Thus, any attack that didn't get the job done right away was no good. The thieves needed to be neutralized quickly.

"Why don't we just plant casks of gunpowder by the fort's walls late at night and blow them up that way?" A different employee offered a suggestion this time, only to be laughed down by her coworkers.

"How's that supposed to be a new weapon?"

However, Ringo didn't join in the heckling.

It wasn't a terrible suggestion.

All they'd been asked to do was come up with a way to destroy the castle. There was no particular reason they had to use a new armament to do so.

Compared to the prospect of building a massive cannon, the woman's suggestion was far more reasonable. The only issue was the matter of geography.

Their target sat atop a hill. Getting to it meant climbing that mound.

All the trees around the fortress had been cleared, so there was no cover and nowhere to hide. Getting ten barrels' worth of gunpowder up without being spotted simply wasn't a realistic strategy.

Between this workshop's equipment and what this world's people know, I dunno if they're up to the task...

Ringo knew how important it was to give the locals chances to grow. The Prodigies needed to avoid helping them any more than was absolutely necessary. She agreed with Tsukasa about all that. That didn't make the decision to do so any easier, though. As Ringo watched the workers struggle, she felt more and more tempted to offer a hand. However, one person in the meeting paid Ringo's concerns no heed.

"Flash! A light just went on in my head!" Cranberry, who had been staring silently at the projected model that whole time, suddenly let out a shout. "Heh, heh, heh. Wow, I really am a GENIUS. I just thought up a great new weapon as easily as if I were thinking up a menu for tomorrow's breakfast. Sometimes my talents scare even me...!" She clutched her shoulders and trembled with an expression of utter ecstasy and delight.

"*Fur real? You thought of something?*" Bearabbit questioned her.

"But of course. The parameters for this mission are to deal a single crippling blow to the building such that it leaves our foes unwilling to fight.

"The angels' Divine Lightning could do that with ease, but we lack the technology to launch a fire rocket with enough gunpowder loaded in it to destroy the wall. In other words, the true question this mission asks of us is: How can we get enough gunpowder to the top of the hill to blow the fortress open?

"Normally, our enemies would never allow us to pull off such a feat...but my GENIUS secret plan is anything but normal!"

Cranberry's proclamation was met with enthusiastic responses from her colleagues.

"So what's the plan?!"

"We're on tenterhooks here!"

"Heh." Cranberry's nostrils flared out with pride. "We're going to use a fire rocket."

""""...Huh?""""

Everyone else tilted their heads in confusion.

"But wait—you just said it yourself. Fire rockets don't have enough oomph to get the job done on their own, and they can't carry gunpowder far enough to do 'em in that way. Hell, even the army only uses 'em to send signals and scare people off. I'm well aware of that, of course. But don't you underestimate me. A GENIUS's ideas are always one step ahead of the rest of her era!"

Cranberry turned her gaze from the other workers, who were all fired up at being told not to belittle her.

"I need to get CRACKING and go draw up the design. And arrange to have purified gunpowder sent over from the empire! And get in touch with the shipyard and have them assemble it! Ah, things are getting exciting now!"

She whirled around and started to run off.

However, Bearabbit hurriedly stopped her.

"H-hold on a minute! You have to tail us what your idea is!"

"Yeah, that's right! Don't go holding out on us, now!"

"If you tell us your plan, we might be able to help out!"

However—

"No. As a citizen of the empire, I can't go around telling other countries my secrets."

—Cranberry refused their requests and gave her nationality as the reason.

"As a special favor, though, I'll give you a detailed explanation on the day I unveil my creation. That should give you something to look forward to! You will forever remember the day you watched a proud noble change the face of siege warfare! Bwa-ha-ha!" With that, Cranberry flapped her arms like a pair of wings and rushed out of the room like a bird soaring through the sky.

"Aaand there she goes."

"Feels like every time I see her, she's always running off somewhere. It's adorable."

"And you know what? Good for her! Always nice to see kids in high spirits!"

When Cranberry got an idea, she didn't hesitate to act on it.

Kind smiles spread across the workers' faces as they watched the girl restlessly scurry about. They clearly regarded her as a mischievous child.

She had gathered the workers on a whim and abandoned them just as arbitrarily, but all of her colleagues were good-natured enough to take her capriciousness in stride.

"...*Ringo, do you think Cranbeary can pull it off?*"

Ringo answered quietly so only Bearabbit could hear. "I don't know, but..."

Cranberry understood the situation's parameters. With how confident she had sounded, she must have had *some* idea. Ringo couldn't begin to imagine what it was, but when she saw Cranberry bubbling with more energy than it seemed possible for her petite body to contain, a thought had crossed her mind.

It looks like she's having fun…

Ringo could definitely relate to that feeling. Whenever fresh inspiration came to her, she couldn't help but want to implement it immediately. Her whole body heated up, and her emotions grew frantic.

By the looks of it, Cranberry was similar. She and Ringo probably had a lot in common.

"…Well, even if it doesn't work, we'll be there to make sure things don't go too badly."

"Fur sure."

Perhaps Cranberry was going to show them something amazing. Maybe her ideas really were a step ahead of the rest of the era.

Soon Ringo would discover that that hunch of hers…was right on the money.

A week had passed since Cranberry took charge of building the weapon to oust the bandits.

In the interim, the criminals had been running wild over the region around their base.

For one, their counterattack on the punitive unit had left the area's military understaffed. It took the army some time to rebuild their forces, so as a temporary measure, Tsukasa had chosen to evacuate all the civilians in the area. In short, there was nobody to stop the bandits from doing as they pleased.

To them, it must have seemed like an all-you-can-steal buffet of gold, livestock, and food. The unprecedented influx of wealth was making them downright giddy.

"Whew! Hot *damn*, this stuff goes down smooth! I'm tellin' ya, this fancy expensive booze is somethin' else. Bottoms up, boys! Not like we can't afford more!"

The bandits' lean, wolflike leader cheerfully pounded on the heap of coins piled up on their table.

His henchmen replied with cheers.

"Whoo! You're the best, Boss!"

"Don't mind if I do!"

"*Buuurp!* This is the life!"

"Ha-ha, you can say that again!"

The sun was still high in the sky, but they were busy filling their pockets with stolen money, their throats with stolen alcohol, and their bellies with stolen meat.

The crooks were on top of the world. And why wouldn't they be when they could obtain such fabulous wealth while hardly lifting a finger? Plus, the gold and luxurious goods sitting before them weren't the only things they had gained.

"But I gotta say, compared to how stingy the nobles who used to live around here were, the big shots down in the capital sure are a generous bunch. They gave us a fat payday *and* these sweet weapons, and all we had to do was a bit of easy stealing…!"

"This is supposed to be top-of-the-line stuff from the imperial workshops, right? You can't even get your hands on normal-ass flintlocks unless you're with the army takin' over the New World for the emperor, and here we are with guns that have some processing that lets 'em shoot even farther. Headin' abroad and selling these babies is gonna net us a fortune."

"But wasn't the deal that we were supposed to leave them behind once we finished running wild with them?"

"What're you, a lawyer? We were never gonna follow no deal."

"Yeah! Think of how pissed Ma'd be if we wasted a bunch of perfectly good weapons like that. Geh-heh-heh."

Tsukasa had been right. These were no ordinary bandits. They were mercenaries sent by a party who would prefer that the peace between Elm and Freyjagard come to an end.

"Still, there's something I don't get."

"Oh? And what's that, my man?"

"No, it's just… Elm was thrashing us in the war until Grandmaster Neuro managed to broker peace, so why do the nobles want us to go rile them up again?"

"Heh. That's 'cause the empire ain't all the same.

"For starters, Emperor Lindworm wasn't the rightful successor. He took the throne by staging a coup d'état against the last emperor.

"And those Four Grandmasters headin' up his government aren't even imperial aristocrats. They're just people who helped him take over.

"But see, the big shot nobles put a lot of work into suckin' up to the old guard, so they were mighty pissed about the leadership changes.

"That's why they're tryin' to rain on their parade.

"They want noble asses back in those grandmaster seats.

"And hey, who can blame 'em? Anyway, point is: That's why they hired us."

The bandit leader lifted up his rifled imperial prototype flintlock gun.

"Aside from Elm's god or whatever, the only ones who've got the know-how to make weapons like these are Freyjagard's imperial workshops. When Elm finds 'em lying around in our hideout, they'll march straight over to the empire and demand answers. And when they do, that'll mark the beginning of the end for the buddy-buddy mood the two countries got goin' on."

"Ohhh. So that's why they wanted us to leave the guns behind when we bailed."

"Wow, you've got those nobles all figured out! See, this is why you're the boss!"

"Heh. Not that we give a rat's ass about their schemes, mind you. We're just here to take everything we can get our hands on. Our next target's the village to the southwest. We're gonna clean 'em out of everything worth takin'."

"""Hell yeah!"""

The henchmen cheered and clinked their tankards together.

But right when their festivities reached a climax—

"Hey, Boss! We got a problem!"

—the grunt on lookout duty rushed into the room with his face white as a sheet.

"Huh? What's wrong?"

"Those Elm guys are at the bottom of the hill, and they've got something real weird with 'em!"

"Whaddaya mean? Weird how? Use your damn words."

"It's, um... It's weeeeeird, man; I dunno how else to describe it."

"Damn, you're useless. If anything's weird here, it's your brain. Way to ruin our party, Dumbass."

The leader gave the lookout a small thump on the head with his tankard, then pushed him aside and made for the ramparts.

"All right, let's see what they've—"

Before the leader could finish, he looked down over the wall—and let out a dumbfounded whisper.

"...The hell is that thing?"

"What *is* that...?"

"It's huge!"

"Is this what they were cookin' up in the Dulleskoff workshop?!"

The Elm delegation was about seven hundred feet from the bandits' hideout.

All of them, workshop employees and Order of the Seven Luminaries soldiers alike, looked in awe at the device that rose into the blue sky.

Cranberry's weapon, which she had transported there via oxcart, was downright majestic.

They couldn't believe how bizarre it appeared or how massive the thing was. With wheels that were thirty feet in diameter, it was a sight to behold.

Is that...? Ringo was struck speechless.

Is that what I think it is? Fur real? Beside her, Bearabbit was no different.

However, their shock was of a whole different sort than the locals'. They both knew of an old Earth weapon that bore a striking resemblance to Cranberry's invention. This planet was still in the relative equivalent of Earth's Middle Ages, though, so it seemed impossible to behold a weapon that hadn't been invented until World War II.

Ringo and Bearabbit at first discounted the resemblance as only superficial. There was no way it could really be what they suspected. Right?

Cranberry spoke proudly, oblivious to Ringo's cold sweating.

"Ha-ha! Behold, the revolutionary new weapon crafted by the GENIUS mind of yours truly!

"As you all know, fire rockets are sorely lacking when it comes to destructive power. For them to fly through the air, their weight needs to be kept to a minimum, so there's a limit to how much gunpowder they can carry. So what do we do? Why, it's simple! We just don't launch them into the air at all!"

She gave one of the massive wheels that made up the giant thing's body a thump.

"By installing twenty fire rockets on each wheel and forty rockets in total, their propulsive power combines to allow delivery of a gigantic, unmanned explosive payload! This is a siege weapon that stands a step ahead of its era, concocted by what will someday be recognized as the finest mind in the empire! I call it—the Great Panjandrum!!"

It really is the Panjandrum!

I can bearly believe it!

Ringo's face went pale, and a large WARNING sign began flashing on Bearabbit's monitor.

Cranberry's humongous ox-driven weapon had a sizeable bomb loaded into its middle and was fashioned with a rocket-laden wheel on each side. It looked like a bobbin from a sewing machine, and just as the two had surmised from its appearance, it was precisely the same sort of armament that Britain had devised during World War II.

Cranberry had done exactly as Ringo predicted. She had crafted a tool far beyond the knowledge of her time.

That isn't just a step ahead of its era, it's centuries ahead...but still!

So then, why was Ringo so terrified? The answer was quite simple.

Back on Earth, the Panjandrum was famous for being one of the most *disastrous creations ever devised*.

The mechanisms behind it were hardly complicated.

When you set off the rockets, their propulsive power made the wheels turn, causing the Panjandrum to barrel forward at speeds of over sixty miles per hour. Upon impact with a target, the large bomb strapped to its center would detonate, causing the enemy's pillbox or trench to go up in smoke. It was basically an overland naval mine.

On paper, it was (supposedly) both highly efficient and extremely practical.

Back on Earth, Britain hoped that it would serve as a trump card that would let them break through the German fortifications during the Normandy landings while keeping friendly casualties to a minimum, and they expended a tremendous amount of money try-ing to develop it.

However, it wasn't long before they ran into trouble. Whenever they tested a prototype, even the slightest bumps in its path would cause it to start going in circles.

Furthermore, it became clear that if the thrust from the rockets on each side wasn't equal, the Panjandrum would veer from its target and trundle off into the night.

The British did their level best to try to straighten out their new problem child, of course. Regrettably, every improvement they made in hopes of getting the Panjandrum ready failed.

On a fundamental level, its design necessitated that its wheels travel along the ground. Hence, no matter how hard any engineer tried, they were never able to fix its incompatibility with rough terrain.

After more mishaps than they could count, the British started coming up with truly pigheaded solutions, like having a soldier run ahead and spread a carpet all the way up to the enemy's pillbox for the Panjandrum to travel across—a fix that defeated the very purpose of using an unmanned explosive. It was around then that they finally returned to their senses and shelved the misguided invention for good.

Such was the heroic tale of Earth's Panjandrum.

The story of this ill-fated contraption left some wondering why anyone would ever think to roll a bomb. Rockets existed, so it seemed more prudent to have a missile ferry the bomb instead. Such notions were perfectly valid.

However, cheese wheels roll. Stones roll. Perhaps the Brits thought it was only natural that bombs should be able to roll as well.

Another theory is that the Panjandrum wasn't a weapon at all, but a flaming chariot *youkai* from Japan that went to Britain by accident, but it was unclear if that theory held any water.

Regardless…

"If she tries to use that, there's no tailing how grizzly things will get…!"

"Bearabbit…!"

"P-pawger that! I'll go tell her that it won't work!"

Ringo signaled Bearabbit with her eyes, and Bearabbit rushed over to try to stop Cranberry. However—

"Cranbeary, I'm sorry to be the bearer of bad news after you put in all that work, but—"

"Hey, I get it! By attaching the fire rockets to the wheels, it makes 'em all sorta go in the same direction!"

"It can totally carry that bomb now!"

"What a stoke of brilliance, thinking of using the fire rockets like that…!"

"And because the whole weapon rolls, it's easy to transport, too!"

"Heh-heh. You HUMDRUM MASSES might be soft in the head, but not me. Now, if you finally understand the magnificence of the soon-to-be head of the imperial workshops, you can show your reverence by calling me Professor!"

"Whoa! You're the best, Professor!"

"You wear a shit-eating grin like nobody else can, Professor!"

"So smug! So cute! So Professor!"

Ringo's and Bearabbit's objections went unnoticed. The Panjandrum's design was very easy to comprehend, and it quickly earned the workers' and soldiers' approval. They showered its inventor with wholehearted applause.

"Th-they all seem so excited that I can bearly bring myself to bruin it for them…!"

"Urgh…"

Bearabbit was right. It was hard to tell them the Panjandrum was defective when the mood was that exultant. Ringo was shy to begin with, so that went double for her.

Yet between workshop staff and soldiers, there were nearly fifty people present.

If the Panjandrum went out of control, people could die.

The weapon itself might have been a joke, but its ability to kill was anything but.

Knowing that—

"U-um!!!!"

—Ringo let out a cry using every last drop of air in her lungs.

Seeing as the exclamation came from a girl who often remained quiet, many of those gathered turned to see what was happening.

"Now then, time to show the world just how magnificent the Panjandrum really is!" Cranberry declared, earning another round of applause.

"Oh…"

Ringo's voice had failed to reach the girl in time. Cranberry cut the rope connecting the Panjandrum to the oxcart.

Having lost its support, the Panjandrum slowly began rolling down the gentle slope in front of them. When it did, the cords attached to the fire rockets in its wheels were ripped out, and the friction caused an immediate reaction with the purified gunpowder contained in the missiles. Sparks and smoke began gushing from all forty of them.

"Thar she blows!"

"They're probably quaking in their boots just looking at it!"

"Feels like it's moving kinda slow, though, doesn't it?"

The workers tilted their heads as they watched the Panjandrum plod languidly along.

"The BOORISH RABBLE are quick to jump to conclusions, I see." Cranberry dismissed their concerns. "Just like a millstone, it needs a lot of torque to get moving at first, but once it gets going—it *goes*!"

The words had barely left Cranberry's mouth when the momentum the Panjandrum had built up on the small decline began paying off. Flames spurted from its rockets as it accelerated forward at a blistering clip. Even once it started making its way up the slope toward the bandits' stronghold, it didn't slow for a moment. If anything, it sped up even more.

"D-damn, that thing can *move!*"

"It's shooting off fire and barreling up that hill like it's nothing!"

"That's thanks to its meticulous lightweight design and the purified gunpowder straight from the imperial workshops! A mound like that is a mere molehill before my Panjandrum! Soldiery types, get yourselves ready to storm the building!"

"""Yes ma'am!"""

The Seven Luminaries forces followed Cranberry's orders and rushed after the Panjandrum, which by that point had become a bona fide horror of smoke and conflagration.

Faced with such a terrifying sight, the thieves—

"AHHHHHHH! WHAT THE HELL IS THAT THING?!"

"I-it's a monster! The wheel monster's coming for us!"

—completely panicked.

It was hard to blame them. After all, there was a pair of wheels thirty feet in diameter spewing crimson and barreling toward them like a raging bull. Even without knowing what the weapon was capable of, it was so menacing that it almost didn't matter.

"Dunno what that thing is, but it looks like bad news…! Mortar it down!"

"Can't! That contraption's too fast! There's no time to load!"

"Tch!"

The bandit leader clicked his tongue at his flustered men, then leaned out over the rampart wall himself and fired at the Panjandrum with his flintlock rifle.

His subordinates followed his lead, taking aim and shooting at the mobile bomb racing up the hill toward them. To something as massive as Cranberry's Panjandrum, though, their bullets were no more than pebbles.

"It's useless! Useless! Useless! You think my craftsmanship is so shoddy I'd let a measly bullet or two blow it up?!"

The explosive at the center of Cranberry's Panjandrum was enclosed in a double-layered iron case. Small external shocks couldn't detonate it. The Panjandrum wasn't going to burst until it hit the fortress walls.

Among the onlookers, none were more astonished by the weapon's performance than Ringo and Bearabbit.

"R-Ringo… I can bearly believe it myself, but is this going to work?!"

"I-it might… I'm just as surprised as you are…"

Things were going far better than either of them could have possibly expected.

As the two thought, they recalled that the Panjandrum's weakness to unstable terrain had only been a problem back on Earth because the British had wanted to use it on the wet, sandy beaches of Normandy.

Any pair of wheels could end up spinning wildly in an environment like that. Perhaps Ringo and Bearabbit were witnessing the failed experiment's redemption?

No sooner did Ringo begin to hope than disaster struck. A stray shot from one of the bandits hit a rocket coupled to one of the wheels by sheer chance. The impact detonated the thing's gunpowder—

"Huh?"

"Hey, wait, it's turning away from the—"

—and the whole wheel sprung up into the air, throwing off the Panjandrum's delicate balance. It swiveled away from its fortress target as though suffering a change of heart.

*　　*　　*

"AHHH! IT'S COMING BACK OUR WAY!!!!"

Ah, there it is.
Paw, there it is.
Then the Panjandrum made a beautiful U-turn and charged back down the hill toward its former allies, picking up speed as it went.

A freak accident? Maybe. But for Ringo and Bearabbit, this was what they'd been anticipating from the start.

After all, one of the most famous stories about the Panjandrum detailed how a group of British officers came to observe one of its test runs, only to have it turn and charge right at them. Barreling off in the wrong direction was in its nature; Britain was the homeland of British Invasion music, and the nation's child, the Panjandrum, was a rebel through and through.

Hoping that something like that would follow orders was just asking for trouble.

As one saying went, it wasn't over until the fat lady sang. And as another described, it wasn't over until the Panjandrum royally screwed everything up.

If anything, the scene unfolding was simply order returning to the universe. It filled Ringo and Bearabbit with a strange sense of relief. The workshop employees and soldiers who had been following the bomb up the hill did not have the benefit of this context, however. So instead, they simply screamed.

"Everyone, fall baaaack! It's going to run us over!"

"Ahhhhhhhhhhhhhhhhh!!!!"

"Hey, Professor! What's the big idea?!"

"It's gonna blow *us* up!"

"Everyone, calm yourselves!!"

As the workers and soldiers panicked, the Panjandrum's inventor, Cranberry, spoke in a dignified tone.

"If you just follow my GENIUS orders, everything will be fine! Now, calm yourselves!"

"I knew you wouldn't let us down, Professor!"

"So cute! So reliable!"

"What do we do?!"

"Why, it's simple! We just c-c-c-calm—calm down, then let it pass over us! If we all dig together, we'll make it in time!"

"Oh no, she's lost it!"

"Noooo! Professor, why?! Right when we needed you most!"

"I gotta say, though, she looks super adorable shoveling through the dirt like that!"

"She totally does, but more importantly, ruuuuun!"

Cranberry's eyes spun as she scraped away at the ground with her little hands, and everyone else took that as their cue to flee from the oncoming horror.

Amid the terror, Ringo and Bearabbit stayed put.

"Bearabbit!"

"Pawger that! Firing resonance bolt!"

On Ringo's orders, Bearabbit launched an eight-inch-long stake out of the large backpack that comprised his body. The thing burrowed into the ground in front of the Panjandrum and the billowing cloud of dust it was kicking up.

Immediately, all the *byuma* present contorted their faces in pain. It was like someone had just stabbed needles in their eardrums.

They looked at Bearabbit's stake, and to their surprise—

"Huh?! The ground's...sinking?!"

—they found a huge sandy pit forming on the verdant hill.

That had been caused by a resonance bolt, one of the many tools

Bearabbit had at his disposal. Ringo had invented the object to demolish earth and bedrock using powerful vibrations.

Due to how handy the resonance bolts were for excavation work in spaces where the differences in atmospheric pressure made traditional explosives harder to use, they were known back on Earth as Moon Moles.

Bearabbit had used one to cave in a large section of the ground right in the Panjandrum's path.

Unable to turn on its own volition, the Panjandrum drove directly into the trap. Then it stopped in its tracks.

Such an outcome was unavoidable.

Despite being equipped with rockets, the Panjandrum ultimately derived its propulsion from its frictional resistance with the ground.

Now that its footing had been reduced to a fine powder, and it had no way to get a decent grip, its flame-spewing wheel merely spun in place.

Unable to move forward, the ill-fated contraption sank deeper and deeper into the sandy pit's grasp, the weight of its gunpowder pulling it down.

Eventually, its rockets burned through the last of their fuel, and the Panjandrum came to a stop.

"I-it's over…"

"We're saved…!"

The workers and soldiers collapsed to the ground with relief.

Off in the distance, they could hear the bandits' jeers.

"Ha-ha-ha-ha-ha! What a hoot! The hell you guys doin' over there?! I mean, it takes a special breed of dumbass to nearly get run over by their own damn weapon. This is what happens when you try to take the easy way out, numbnuts!"

"Ga-ha-ha-ha! What a bunch of losers!"

"……!" Cranberry's slender shoulders trembled at their mockery.

Poor thing..., thought Ringo.

Cranberry was still down on all fours with her head hung. Worried, Ringo wanted to offer her some compassionate words, but she never got the chance.

"Boss, the mortar's ready to go!"

"That's what I like to hear. Let's give those know-it-all dimwits a little taste of what war is like."

A projectile came jutting out over the top of the ramparts.

Ringo and Bearabbit immediately realized the danger they were in.

If one of those shells hit the Panjandrum's payload, they could all go up in smoke.

Bearabbit grabbed Ringo with his manipulator arms, tossed her on his back—

"*E-everyone, fall back to the town! I'll retrieve the new weapon later, so fur now, just turn tail and run!*"

—and urged the others to take shelter.

"G-got it!"

The workers nodded, and one of them grabbed Cranberry's arm and tried to help her up.

"Come on, Cranberry! We need to get out of here!"

"~~~~~~~~~~~!!"

However, Cranberry shook the woman's hand right off. Then she got up on her own and ran toward the town. It was hardly an admirable way to respond to her coworker's concern. Still, no one thought worse of her for it. During the brief moment she turned around and looked back, they had all seen her face.

"She was crying, wasn't she...?"

Cranberry's eyes were wet, her face was flushed, and her eyebrows were drooping in defeat. The girl looked ready to break at the slightest touch.

"Makes sense. She's got skills, but she's just a kid. The poor thing was probably scared stiff!"

"Worry about that later and run!"

It wouldn't be fair of the workshop employees or the soldiers to expect a child to control her emotions. As adults, it was their job to forgive her.

"........."

Ringo watched Cranberry dash ahead with an entirely different sentiment, though.

In order to escape the runaway Panjandrum and any possible pursuit from the bandits, Ringo and the others fled all the way to a nearby town.

With Bearabbit manning the rear and intercepting any mortar fire from the bandits, everyone made it out with minor injuries. It was only when the immediate danger had passed that someone realized an important person was missing.

"Huh? Wait, where's Cranberry?"

At some point, Cranberry Diva had disappeared.

"M-maybe she fell behind...?!"

"Nah, that ain't it. She was still up in front of us when we came through the town gate."

"Perhaps she didn't know where we were staying and got lost or something."

"That could be it...or maybe she's so embarrassed her experiment went south that she doesn't want to face us."

"C'mon, she should know that none of us hold it against her..."

As the workers stood in front of the inn fretting about Cranberry, Bearabbit approached them.

"If you want, I can—"

He was about to offer to use his divine gift, his satellite imaging, to track her down.

"Bearabbit…" Ringo, who was standing beside the robot, cut him off, though.

"Hmm?"

"W-we should all go search for her. We gotta find Cranberry before the sun goes down."

"Yeah, that's right. Don't want to leave a kid alone in a strange town."

"Let's split up and find her!"

Before Bearabbit had a chance to finish making his offer, the workshop staff all went off in different directions, looking for their missing coworker.

Bearabbit turned to Ringo in the now-deserted area in front of the inn. *"Ringo, why'd you stop me? With our satellite, I could have found Cranberry's pawsition in no time."*

He was right. There was no need to have everyone split up and hunt for her on foot. Obviously, Ringo knew that the satellite could resolve this in mere moments, and she had an answer to Bearabbit's reasonable inquiry.

"If it were me… I wouldn't want to see the others right now."

However, Ringo also understood that Cranberry's colleagues had misunderstood. They thought she had gotten lost because she was a child. Everyone had assumed her screwup left her too embarrassed to show her face.

Ringo knew that Cranberry wasn't nearly as much of a kid as the others believed. The genius inventor turned to Bearabbit with a serious look in her eyes.

"Tell me where she is."

"......*Hic.*"

As the workshop staff scoured the town, Cranberry hid behind a row of empty wine barrels in a back alley a little ways from the inn and choked back tears.

She had made a terrible error. After all that boasting, things had gone awry. Worst of all...Cranberry had endangered everyone.

If Ringo the angel and Bearabbit hadn't been there to bail her out, there was no telling how bad things could have gone.

The workshop staff was probably livid with her. Surely, they had to be thinking that none of this would've happened if Cranberry hadn't gotten so full of herself. Imagining how her colleagues saw her filled the girl with fear. She didn't dare face them.

Suddenly, the melancholy girl heard someone.

"Cranberry?"

"Ah!"

"You're...back here...right?"

Cranberry turned toward the large barrel behind her. Someone was calling to her from the road. The voice belonged to a girl, but it was unfamiliar. It didn't belong to any of Cranberry's coworkers. However, the fact that the girl was looking for Cranberry meant she must have had some connection to her.

Not ready to face the music yet, Cranberry devised an idea to throw off her pursuer.

"*M-meow...*"

She tried getting her to leave her alone by pretending to be a cat.

It was a stunningly good impression, unfortunately—

"Oh, a kitty. ♡"

—the mimicry only brought the person closer.

I-it backfired!

Cranberry panicked and started to stand, hoping to make a run for it, but it was already too late.

Riku Misora

When the speaker—Ringo Oohoshi, one of the Seven Luminaries' angels and the head of the Elm workshops—popped her head up over the barrel and found Cranberry hiding there, a brief flash of disappointment crossed her face at not having discovered a cat. She quickly corrected her expression, though, giving Cranberry a gentle smile.

"…You're a pretty big kitty."

"Ah…"

Cranberry rose to her feet. Thoroughly embarrassed after being discovered in such a manner, she made up her mind to flee. The plan was to slip past Ringo and escape down the road. However, the moment she leaned forward—

"If you go out now…the others…will find you."

"_____!"

"They're worried…about you…so they're all…out looking."

—Ringo gave her a quiet warning.

Cranberry stood still for a moment and finally heard the voices of those searching for her. They weren't far. If she'd left the alley, she might very well have crashed right into them. Running would do her no good now.

"I-I'm really sorry about all this. I'll come with you in a minute…"

"It's fine…if you're not…ready yet. Really."

"Huh?"

Cranberry was shocked to hear that. If Ringo hadn't come to retrieve her, then what was she doing here?

As Cranberry considered that question in puzzlement, Ringo took advantage of her slight frame to slip behind the barrel and slide down next to the other girl. She opened up the thermos hanging from her shoulder. Then she poured some of the steamy beverage from within into a cup and offered it to Cranberry.

"Would you…like some? It's milk coffee…with lots of sugar.

41

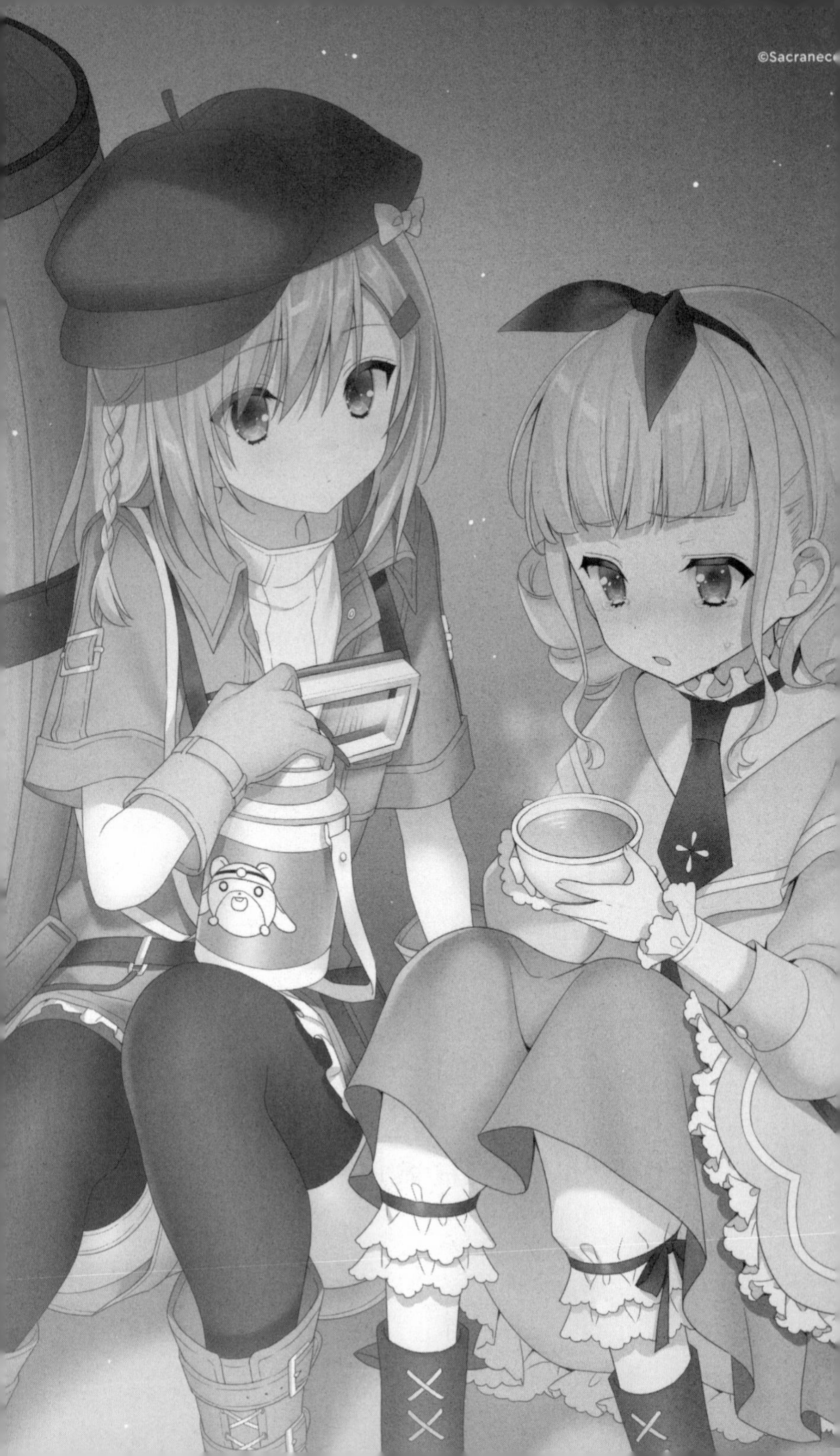
©Sacranec

Drinking it...always helps me compose myself when I'm feeling down."

"...Th-thank you."

Cranberry took the steaming coffee. The girl didn't even want it all that much, but she did so on reflex. A sad, silent laugh escaped her lips. Even she could tell that she wasn't thinking straight. However, Cranberry knew that it would be far too rude to give the drink back at this point.

She sipped the coffee.

It was a little hot, but it was sweet, too. Cranberry had heard of this new beverage brought over from the New World, but she'd never imagined it was something so tasty.

Its taste slowly but surely warmed her pained heart.

"...I'm pathetic, aren't I? After all that boasting, I screwed up and put everyone in danger... And then, to top it all off, I got so scared of getting blamed for my mistake that I ran off. I've been acting like a child."

When someone felt truly cornered, they didn't have the focus to complain like that. Cranberry probably had the milk coffee to thank for her being collected enough to be self-deprecating.

Ringo had something to say about that, though.

"...That's not...it, is it?"

"Huh?"

"You're not scared of getting blamed for your mistake. You're frightened they'll forgive you *because they think of you as a child*."

"!"

The statement took Cranberry's breath away. Ringo had hit the nail on the head. Cranberry would have been fine with taking responsibility for her failure *as an inventor*.

However...

"...You're totally right, Ms. Angel. I came here to learn about engineering as a representative of the empire. I can't let them look down on me like that!"

The exchange student program was highly competitive. For every person who got in, there were a hundred more who hadn't. Those were the kinds of odds that Cranberry had overcome to get where she was.

As one of the empire's few representatives, her country's future depended on her ability to learn about the angels' strange technology and bring that knowledge back with her. There was a tremendous amount of responsibility resting on her small shoulders. That was why she couldn't let them make light of her or think of her as immature.

If others looked down on her and excluded her from projects because of her age, then she wouldn't be able to fulfill her duty. Cranberry had beaten out plenty of adults to win her spot in the exchange program, so she needed to be able to stand on the same level they would have.

That was why she had tried so incessantly to play up how brilliant she was. In the world of adults, her age was an obstacle that needed to be overcome. Unfortunately, none of her coworkers had appreciated that. They'd remained ignorant of her responsibilities, of the struggle of being a child who had to stand shoulder to shoulder with adults.

Undoubtedly, Cranberry's colleagues would forgive her. They would tell her not to worry about it and assure her that it was natural for kids to screw up. Cranberry knew all that. And that was why she ran away. It was her only choice.

When Cranberry thought about hearing those cruel words, it hurt so bad it made her want to cry.

"...I guess I shouldn't be surprised. It makes sense that someone like you can read people's minds."

Ringo shook her head. "I can't...do anything like that. I was just... in a similar situation...myself."

"You were...?"

Ringo nodded, then began awkwardly explaining.

She told Cranberry about how she had been a manufactured genius. While the other girl listened intently, Ringo recounted her receiving special teachings from her mother and how she had worked as a researcher in world-class laboratories from a young age. Thankfully, Ringo made sure to leave enough details fuzzy so it wouldn't call her identity as an angel into question.

Just like Cranberry, Ringo had been thrust into the world of adults as a kid. Although America, the country she spent much of her childhood in, had accepted her genius with open arms, that didn't change the fact that, wherever she went, she was always the youngest person around.

Ringo could remember all too well what it was like not to have any friends her own age and to constantly push herself to avoid sullying her influential mother's name. She had been smart enough to recognize how her own failures reflected on others.

"So I know how it feels...to think you have to push yourself... And how much...it hurts...when you screw up..."

"...That's quite a surprise." Cranberry made no efforts to conceal her shock at Ringo's confession.

Ringo and the other angels may have looked human, but due to how otherworldly their technology was, Cranberry had always assumed they were some sort of enlightened beings. She never considered that they could struggle the same ways humans could. Yet since they did...there was something Cranberry needed to know.

"So um, Ms. Angel...what did you do? How did you recover when you messed up something important and felt scared to go back because everyone else thought you were just a kid playing around?"

"I..." Ringo had to think for a minute before answering. "I'm... sorry. I don't really...know."

"Huh?"

"I did...pretty much the same thing...you did. When I made mistakes...I would get miserable...and hide from everyone and drink coffee like this...and space out... But then I would always stumble upon some new idea I wanted to try out, and before long, that would be the only thing I could think about... Before I knew it, I was back in the lab researching. I just really like...making things."

People had treated Ringo like a kid, mocked her, and said terrible things to her throughout her life. However, once that switch inside her flipped, *none of that bothered her anymore*. Once inspiration took hold, all she thought about was realizing her new idea.

Over time, those around her started changing. At some point, all the adults stopped seeing Ringo as the mere child she appeared to be. When her coworkers looked at her then, they did so with gazes full of envy, awe, and respect. Even so, Ringo couldn't point to a single moment that sparked that change.

"So like...I said... I genuinely don't know," Ringo said apologetically. She didn't have the quick fix that Cranberry was looking for that would get her right back on her feet.

Near as Ringo could figure, every time she was down, she eventually got engrossed in work again. Before long, she was back in her lab and had forgotten about her troubles.

"I'm...sorry. I wish I could give you...better advice, but...I'm kind of clueless...about everything except my work..."

If Ringo were Tsukasa or Masato, perhaps she may have given Cranberry fantastic instructions on how to manage her interpersonal relationships, yet she wasn't. The genius inventor looked down in shame. Running to help because she saw a younger employee who suffered as she once had was noble, but it didn't count for much without any decent advice to give.

Yet astonishingly—

"Not at all. That was very educational."

—Cranberry thanked Ringo.

Somehow, her voice sounded more stalwart than it had a moment ago. Surprised by the change, Ringo took a peek at Cranberry's face. All the gloom from just before had vanished.

"...I realize now that my responsibilities made me pay a little too much attention to how people saw me. After all, I *am* twelve, so it only makes sense that they would treat me like a kid. Still, it was laughably foolish of me to let their evaluations cause me to doubt my skills. Besides...I already overcame droves of the empire's best and brightest just getting here!"

That success alone was proof of Cranberry's intelligence. And with that feather in her cap, what could she possibly have to fear? People might mock her and call her a child or laugh at her mistakes. But as long as Cranberry believed in her ideas and treated her brilliance as a foregone conclusion...

"...Then in time, people will stop treating me like a juvenile all on their own!" proclaimed Cranberry as she stood. "Now, back to the inn! It's an inventor's job to forge a miracle out of the towering scrap heap of their mistakes, so I don't have a minute to waste dawdling here!"

"You're...okay?" Ringo was concerned that Cranberry was just putting on a brave face, but the girl replied by flashing her the *V* for *victory* hand sign and beaming from ear to ear.

"Of course I am; I'm a GENIUS! The word *impossible* isn't even in my vocabulary!"

When Ringo saw Cranberry's unreserved smile, she breathed a small sigh of relief. "Glad...to hear it."

Things hadn't played out quite the way Cranberry had expected, but the fact remained that the Panjandrum was a weapon of the future. There was no doubt in Ringo's mind that anyone who could not only think up such a device in this more primitive era, but build it to completion in a mere week, would prove to be an invaluable asset to that world.

Someday, once the Prodigies were gone, Cranberry might well be the one driving this world to industrial greatness.

The truth of the matter was: The seven high schoolers from Earth had given the people a little too much advanced technology, even though doing so had been necessary for the new nation to win its independence. Tsukasa was worried about how far ahead of its neighbors Elm was, and Ringo shared his concerns.

If other countries were going to bridge that gap, they couldn't let themselves give up after a single minor setback. Doing so would be a crying shame. That was why Ringo felt relieved that Cranberry was back in high spirits. However, nothing could have prepared her for the girl's proud follow-up.

"And because it was conceived of by a GENIUS mind, it stands to reason that the Panjandrum must be an amazing weapon after all!"

"…Huh?"

"There are still some kinks to work out, of course, and we ran into some bad luck this time around, but the Panjandrum has yet to show off its true power! All it needs is a little elbow grease and ingenuity!"

"No, I really don't…think that's—"

"WHOOOOOA! I figured it out! I suddenly came up with the idea that will turn bitter failure into brilliant success! I—I have to get back! I've got a long, tea-fueled night ahead of me!"

"H-hold on a—" Panicking, Ringo tried to stop Cranberry, but just as she herself had pointed out, the two had a lot in common. That included the part about not paying attention to anything else once an idea popped into their minds.

As Cranberry was now, Ringo's quiet voice had no chance of

stopping her. The girl rushed out of the alleyway and raced toward the inn with her arms extended like wings. Although Ringo was glad that Cranberry had rediscovered her confidence, she hadn't expected it to take such a dramatic turn.

In a way, Cranberry almost resembled the Panjandrum herself.

For some reason, Ringo felt a vague unease nip at her heart. Perhaps she ought not to have said all she had. It may have only succeeded in throwing oil on the fire. A lukewarm sweat trickled down her back at the thought.

And a mere five days later…

…Ringo's premonition came true.

"""AHHHHHHHHHHHHHHHHH!!!!""""

A roar loud enough to shake a mountain rose to the sky above Buchwald province, accompanied by a raucous chorus of bandit screams.

Black smoke billowed up from the ravaged fortress, and the Elm soldiers poured into the wreckage and subdued the panicked outlaws with ease.

At first, one may have thought that Bearabbit was responsible for this, but that was incorrect. Believe it or not, it was the Panjandrum.

"Ringo, that was…"

"Yeah… She used a winch…"

After watching the whole thing play out, Ringo and Bearabbit were sure of it.

A winch was a rotating drum that wound a rope, and there were two primary ways to employ it. One was to fix the winch in place, and the other was to set the rope.

Both options had their purposes. For instance, the former was often used when anchoring seacraft, and the latter was handy for getting off-road trucks over and around obstacles by affixing the other end of the winch to a tree or something similar.

Cranberry had adopted the second method.

She had constructed a new Panjandrum even lighter than the original prototype, and after using a massive siege ballista to fire an anchor at the fortress, she had set it up so that the Panjandrum's independent propulsion wound up the long rope attached to the anchor. No matter how hard it tried to abandon its course, the winding process meant that it would eventually make its way to the target at the end of its rope.

Thanks to Cranberry's superior technical skills, the field test went off without a hitch. Even though the Panjandrum fell onto its side partway up the hill, the wound rope's strength got it to the finish line anyway. Once there, it successfully blasted the old bastion's ramparts to smithereens.

"Ha-ha-ha! How do you like *them* apples?! This is what you get when you put a GENIUS on the job! I told you not to underestimate me!"

"Whoo! You go, Professor!"

"I said it before, and I'll say it again—you wear a shit-eating grin like nobody else can, Professor!"

"Ha-ha! Praise me more!"

Having made good on her promise to destroy the bandits' hideout, Cranberry puffed up her little chest as far as it would go with the smuggest expression imaginable. As she did, her coworkers gathered around and celebrated her talents by lavishing her with compliments and applause. Even the soldiers got in on it, inquiring when Cranberry could start mass-producing Panjandrums.

As she basked in adoration, Cranberry boldly replied that she would make newer, even better Panjandrums by the dozens and forever change the face of war.

Ringo watched the situation rapidly reach the point of no return. Visions of the tricked-out Panjandrums that would no doubt soon come into being danced through her head as a painful realization finally struck her.

She really wasn't cut out for this mentorship stuff.

❦ Inviting Unrest ❦

"Pray, forgive this sudden visit… I am Empress Kaguya of the Yamato Empire. As ye Seven Luminaries and your Republic of Elm *promote the doctrine of equality for all*, I have come seeking salvation for my country, now oppressed by the wicked Freyjagard Empire. If ye would remain true to your convictions, then might ye find it in your hearts to aid us?"

After a mysterious plane crash, the Seven High School Prodigies found themselves in another world.

It was only thanks to the good people of Elm Village that they survived, and the Prodigies chose to repay that kindness by helping them fight to win their safety and freedom.

They did so by borrowing the name of this planet's ancient Seven Luminaries' religion. After some hardships, they managed to wrest independence from the hands of the ruling Freyjagard Empire and successfully founded the Republic of Elm.

Afterward, the septet made peace with the empire and signed a treaty with a one Grandmaster Neuro ul Levias—a man who, like them, originally hailed from another world.

Then, through a trade conference with Freyjagard and several other foreign nations, they issued their new goss currency and thus solidified their young republic as a full-fledged country.

Now the Prodigies were beginning their final major undertaking. With Elm solid and able to stand on its own two feet, it was time for the seven high schoolers to hold national elections to transfer power over to the native inhabitants of this planet. However, the moment they tried to announce the news to the whole of their country via broadcasting "obelisks," a pair of young women crashed their event.

The two of them leaped over the crowd astride a massive white wolf and landed atop the stage where Prodigy politician Tsukasa Mikogami was announcing the election.

One of the interlopers was the light-haired *byuma* Shura, who had previously rescued the Prodigies back in Freyjagard. The other had dark hair and claimed to be the princess of the now-defunct nation of Yamato.

Prodigy businessman Masato Sanada clicked his tongue from beside the stage.

"Tch. Well, ain't this a fine mess…"

"Huh? What? Masato, you know what's going on?"

Masato gave Prodigy magician Prince Akatsuki's bewildered question a succinct answer.

"She's using our public stance against us."

"Our what?"

"We employed the noble cause of 'equality for all' to unite the masses, so the chick's holding the legitimacy of our claim hostage to pressure us into saving her country from its invaders, too. And because of our standing, we're in no position to turn her down."

"H-how's that?"

"'Cause as the Seven Luminaries, we don't have any good reason to. If we ignore her plea, then the people'd start wondering why

Yamato isn't included in the idea of equality for *all*. And it gets worse… 'Equality for all' is the backbone we founded our democracy on. If we want Elm to stick around after we're gone, we can't afford to besmirch its fundamental principle here."

If the Prodigies, as the exemplars to the masses and the objects of their devotion, compromised on that philosophy, it would be sure to cast a dark shadow over the nation's future.

But on the other hand, if they accepted her request, it'd be like declaring war on Freyjagard all over again. Their hard-won cease-fire with the empire would have been for naught. Worse, Masato feared it ran the risk of souring their relationship with Grandmaster Neuro.

Not only was Neuro from another world like the Prodigies, but he also held the only method they knew of to get back to Earth. The seven high schoolers didn't want to get on his bad side. They couldn't afford to.

How you gonna play this, Tsukasa? wondered Masato.

"I implore ye, oh angels. Just as when ye fought the empire for Elm's sake, it is now Yamato that hath need of your strength. Canst ye afford to refuse our plea if ye would stand by your ideal of equality for all?"

Once again, Kaguya used the Republic of Elm's creed as a weapon to strong-arm Tsukasa into agreeing to help liberate the Yamato Empire.

Masato and the other Prodigies waited with bated breath for their leader to give his response. With all eyes on him, Tsukasa gave his answer.

"Whether we help you or not, there's another matter that needs to be addressed first." Then he called out to the soldiers surrounding the stage. "Guards! Arrest these two for the crime of illegal entry!"

"Understood, m'lord! To arms!"

""""Yes ma'am!"""""

When Tsukasa gave the order, Prodigy swordmaster Aoi Ichijou rushed onto the stage and leveled her blade at the intruders. The soldiers around her followed the young woman's lead and aimed their guns at the two intruders and the wolf.

"Freeze! Drop your weapons and put your hands above your head!"

"How cruel. Be it the way of the Seven Luminaries to flog poor lost lambs seeking aid?"

"_____"

"Grrr…!"

The silver-haired *byuma*, Shura, responded to their hostility by stepping in front of Kaguya and reaching for her sword, and the large wolf behind them bared its fangs and growled. It was clear that they had no intention of coming quietly. They were prepared to do battle, if necessary.

Though her opponent's name was Shura, Aoi Ichijou knew that defeating her would be anything *but* sure. She felt the hair on the back of her neck rise.

Aoi had seen Shura fight when the Prodigies had been ambushed on the way back from the peace summit, so she knew exactly how formidable the young woman's skills were. She would have been a fierce opponent at the best of times, and with Aoi's beloved sword Hoozukimaru lost and no suitable replacement yet found, the circumstances could hardly be described as ideal.

If things got violent…

…I shan't emerge unscathed, that I shan't.

With that being the case, Aoi knew she had to protect Tsukasa at all costs.

Aoi was but a vassal. She could be replaced. To lose Tsukasa, however, would be no less than to have their proverbial head chopped off. With her resolve firm, Aoi placed herself between Shura and Tsukasa.

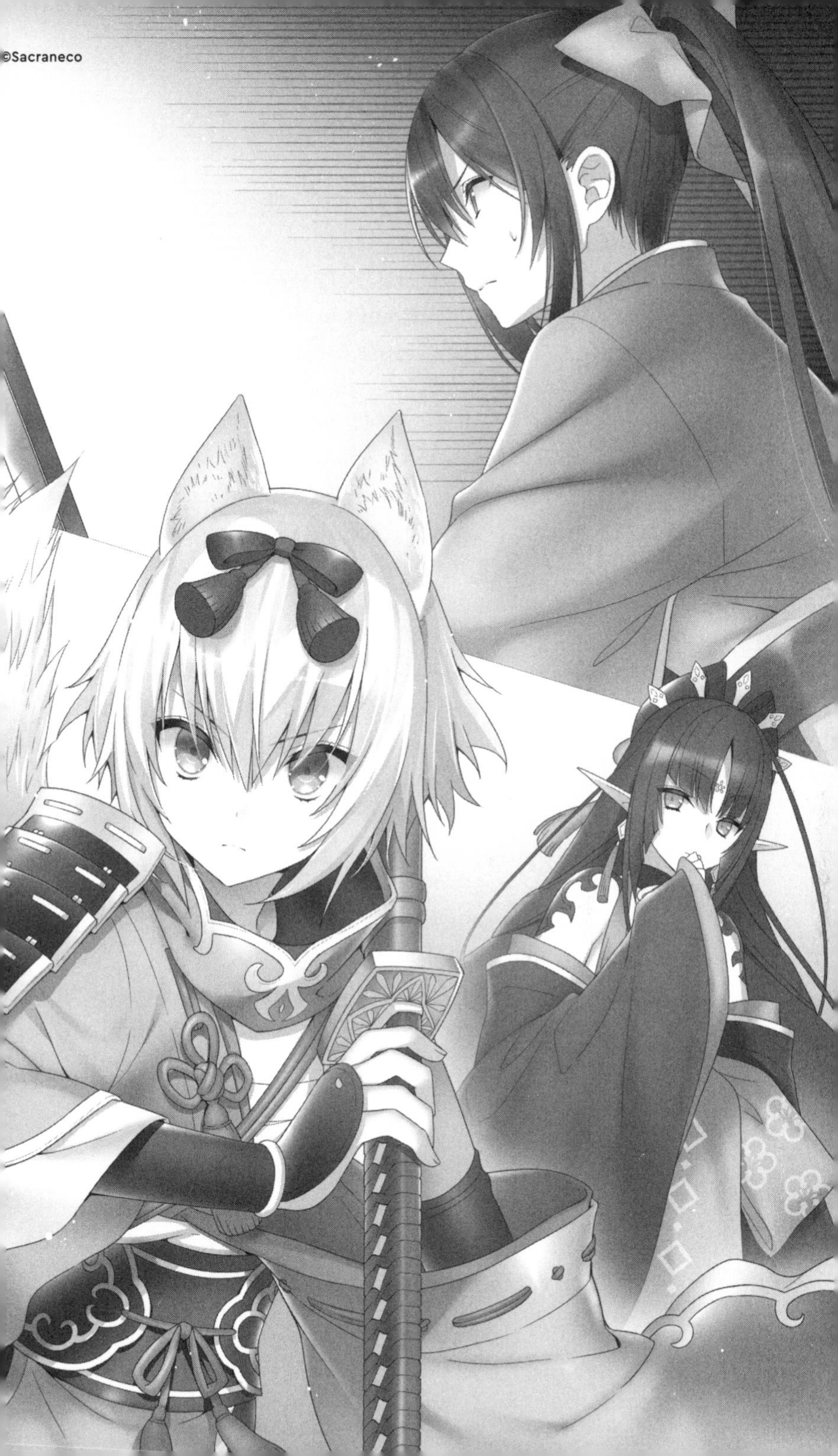

Despite the crackling tension in the air, Tsukasa replied to Kaguya without so much as a hint of alarm or trepidation.

"As I said, this is an issue that has to be resolved before we decide whether we help you. At the moment, we have no proof that you're actually the fugitive Princess Kaguya of the defunct Yamato Empire that you claim to be. As such, yours is not a request we can afford to answer lightly.

"If you were an impostor, doing so would strew unnecessary discord between Freyjagard and us. There could even be negative repercussions for the people of what was once Yamato. And more importantly...even if you are the real Princess Kaguya, I don't recall authorizing you to enter our borders.

"As Elm's secretary of the interior, I go through and check the records of all who have entered or left Elm. If I don't know how you got in, then that's proof enough that you didn't do so through legal channels. That makes you an illegal alien.

"In times like these, a nation must ensure that its laws are upheld and that any who break them face justice. If what you say is true, and you truly are royalty, then I'm sure you understand the position I'm in."

"...So stubborn," Kaguya replied with a shrug and a bitter smile. "Very well. Thy point hath merit."

She raised her hands in the air—the universal sign of surrender.

"Shura, throw down thy weapon."

"...Are you sure?"

Shura cocked her head to the side, and Kaguya nodded.

"All is well. He hath not refused us outright. Besides which...this is a conversation he would rather not have in front of a crowd."

"By your command." Shura obeyed her master's order and dropped her *nodachi* greatsword on the ground, sheath and all. Then she shot a meaningful glance at the wolf baring its fangs behind Kaguya.

"Shiro."

The beast responded by leaving the two young women behind and leaping away. After getting to the roof of one of the buildings surrounding Dulleskoff's central park in a single bound, it continued jumping from the top of one structure to another until the beast made its escape.

"I-it's getting away!"

"Dammit! Follow that wolf!"

When Kaguya saw the Elm soldiers about to race off after it, she gave them a smile and a pithy remark. "Oh? Doth Elm require entry permits of its beasts of the wild, then?"

"...No. No, it does not."

Elm's laws regarding border control didn't extend to animals. Tsukasa took the hint and told his soldiers to stand down.

He knew how foolish it would be to get hung up on a single wolf and risk having the pair of unexpected guests change their minds about surrendering.

Instead, he ordered the soldiers to detain the two young women in a cell in the barracks.

After Kaguya and Shura went along peacefully, the flustered crowd settled down, and the illegal-entry incident ended without a fuss.

"Th-thank goodness... I was afraid we were to get in a fight...," Akatsuki said with a sigh.

"Yeah, that coulda gotten ugly. Good thing our glorious prime minister managed to dodge the issue so smoothly," Masato responded.

Once things calmed down, Tsukasa proceeded as planned and announced to the nation that the Republic of Elm would be holding its inaugural elections. Seeing him stand at that podium as confidently as ever filled Akatsuki with reassurance, a sentiment Masato shared. However...

"This ain't over, though," Masato remarked.

"It's not?" questioned Akatsuki.

"Our man Tsukasa was able to get away with not giving them a clear answer this time around, but thanks to our broadcast, all of Elm got a front-row seat to the debacle. Sooner or later, the Seven Luminaries are gonna have to give her a formal response. She knew that. It's the only reason she left so quietly."

Would the Prodigies save Yamato or forsake it?

Everyone was dying to know how Tsukasa would answer. Try as they might, though, none of them could see through his poker face.

Both Princess Kaguya of the defunct Yamato Empire and Shura the White Wolf General were wanted in the Freyjagard Empire as war criminals. Thus, news of the capture was swiftly sent to the Freyjagard government through their embassy in Elm following the two nations' joint security agreement.

Due to the emperor's absence, the staff member who received the report quickly headed to one of the four people entrusted with managing the nation in his absence—Grandmaster Neuro ul Levias.

"I'm terribly sorry for interrupting you on your holiday, Grandmaster Neuro!"

"I would certainly hope so. I made it *abundantly* clear that I was taking today off." Neuro continued reclining slovenly on his sofa as he replied to the man.

It wasn't even noon yet, but snacks and bottles of liquor had already joined the books and documents on his table. The telltale light of drunkenness accompanied the displeased look in the man's half-open eyes. It would appear that alcohol had featured prominently in Neuro's plans for the day.

"Again, my sincerest apologies. However, I'm here about a

matter of some urgency," the messenger answered. "We just received word from our embassy in Elm that the Seven Luminaries arrested a pair of women claiming to be the notoriously elusive Kaguya and Shura of Yamato on charges of illegal entry. The Seven Luminaries have requested through our ambassador that we help verify their identities, and—"

"…I know."

"What? You've already heard, Lord Grandmaster…?"

Hearing that gave the messenger pause. Who could have reported the news to Neuro before he got there?

Unconcerned with the servant's consternation, Neuro issued orders in a listless, almost exasperated tone. "Someone from our old Yamato embassy can tell whether we're dealing with the actual princess. Go find one and send them up to Elm, although ten to one says she's exactly who she claims to be."

"At once!"

"And if that's all, then scram. I'm in a sour enough mood as it is."

"O-of course, sir! Forgive me!"

The messenger bowed and beat a hasty retreat. After watching him close the door, Neuro heaved a deep sigh.

"Well, this is unfortunate. I hate it when things don't go as planned."

The Yamato survivors had made contact with the Seven High School Prodigies. It was a turn of events that Neuro had been hoping to avoid. Contrary to what he had told the Prodigies, he was no mere immigrant from another world. Neuro was a man with an objective. And those seven being here interfered with his goal.

If possible, he wanted them gone from this planet as soon as could be. He certainly didn't want anyone stirring up any unnecessary commotion. Moreover…

Yamato is where the roots of her *household lie.*

"Does the phrase evil dragon *mean anything to you?"*

"...Should it? Sorry, I don't have any idea what you're talking about."

During Neuro's meeting with the Prodigies, he had concealed the truth from them. Their knowing would lead them to uncover some rather unsavory facts. Should that come to pass, then peacefully resolving things would no longer be an option for Neuro. His relationship with the septet would be damaged beyond repair.

They had only stumbled into this world by accident, but it was clear that they held a sense of responsibility toward it all the same. There was little chance they'd remain idle if they discovered Neuro's true mission.

Perhaps *she* had lost as much of her power as they had. Regardless, the heroes' summoning had been imperfect, and they didn't seem to know why they'd been called here in the first place. Neuro would have been perfectly happy maintaining friendly relations with them, sending them back to their home none the wiser, and then going and capturing the Key Maiden afterward.

I really, really hate it when things don't go as planned.

Violence wasn't his style. It required far too much effort.

This world's primitive inhabitants were one thing, but going up against powerful folks like those seven was a tall ask for Neuro's feeble husk of flesh. He had to make sure it never came to that.

"I guess I can't afford to keep sitting around like this, then." As he murmured to himself, Neuro retrieved a sheet of parchment from his drawer and began composing a letter. It was addressed to Jade von Saint-Germain.

Jade was the man the empire had assigned as the Yamato dominion's administrator to serve as their watchdog. If the Seven Luminaries started poking their noses around Yamato, they would eventually cross his path. In the letter, Neuro gave Jade instructions on what to do if that happened.

As he scribbled across the parchment, Neuro cast his gaze toward the crystal ball sitting among the mess atop his table. An image danced hazily on its dimly glowing surface. It was of a beautiful girl with long blond hair and pointy ears.

There could be no mistaking her.

It was, without a doubt, the girl who had looked after the Prodigies when they first crash-landed in this world—Lyrule.

CHAPTER 1

⚜ Split Path ⚜

A week had passed since the incident with Kaguya.

Prodigy journalist Shinobu Sarutobi was away infiltrating the empire under the guise of being an exchange student. However, the other six High School Prodigies were having lunch in the Republic of Elm's government office building in Dulleskoff with their three closest acquaintances from Elm Village: Lyrule, Elch, and Winona.

Lyrule sighed in her seat.

"This is quite the predicament we're in…"

"You mean with the Yamato princess comin' and asking for help three years after her country went down? Seems like it's all people're talking about these days," Winona replied.

"My staff members are starting to get restless, too. And right after we managed to make peace with the empire…," remarked Elch.

The two echoed Lyrule's concerns. And it wasn't just the people of Elm who were worried about the republic's intruders, either.

"My exchange students from the empire who came to learn about medicine have been on edge as well. Why, they can hardly even focus on their studies," Keine added.

In the students' case, they were scared that the event would worsen Elm and Freyjagard's relationship.

Although unilateral agreements between the two nations guaranteed their safety, it was all too common for such accords to be ignored in times of war. Elm had no intentions whatsoever of doing such a thing, but the students could hardly be blamed for feeling uneasy.

"What about yours, Ringo?" inquired Keine.

"…She…doesn't seem…too worried. But Bearabbit…is another… story…"

"Well, if anyone starts acting oddly, don't hesitate to call. My counseling services are at your disposal."

"…I feel like…it's hard to find anyone…at the workshop…who doesn't act oddly…"

Cranberry's success with the Panjandrum had only served to heighten her arrogance, and Ringo had observed a corresponding uptick in her coworkers' degeneracy. She gave a small, sarcastic laugh. The Prodigy scientist suspected that counseling wouldn't do them much good.

"Yamato, huh. Never thought I'd hear that name again."

"Winona, you got some sorta history with 'em?" Masato asked.

"…Yeah, you could say that. You know how I told you my Adel died from getting caught up in a war? It was the one against Yamato."

"Oh, man."

"Yamato was pretty closed off and didn't produce anything all that impressive, but my old man made big inroads with them for the Orion Company. Even after the fighting started, he headed down there anyway 'cause of all they'd done for him and helped smuggle food and medicine to the civilians who got caught up in the fighting," Elch added.

"Sounds like he was a good man…"

Although Adel's actions technically qualified as aiding the enemy, Akatsuki couldn't help but view them favorably.

However, Winona felt differently. "Like hell he was," she replied indignantly. "What kind of 'good man' dies and leaves such a young, hot, likable, and most importantly, young, widow behind? Jerk's probably burning in hell."

"Mom, I don't wanna say you've got an ego problem, but..."

"Nah, Winona's right. Any guy who'd make a babe as choice as her mourn for him is scum!"

"See, *Masato* gets it, unlike a certain little punk who wouldn't know how to talk to a girl if she hit him over the head. Maybe if you took a page from his book, you could actually get some mileage out of those good looks you inherited from me."

"Piss off!"

Flustered by his own flesh and blood, Elch angrily stuffed his mouth full of bread.

"Heh..." Keine laughed. "Still, Tsukasa, I must say that you handled the situation at the election announcement with aplomb."

"Indeed. He was as cool as a cucumber, that he was," Aoi agreed. "And seeing that helped the citizens keep their composure in turn. Might it be that you knew they were coming, m'lord?"

Tsukasa Mikogami, the person who had arranged the lunch, responded to their inquiring gazes by nodding. "More or less. I didn't know that they would choose that moment to do so, but I was prepared for Yamato to make contact sooner or later."

"You...were?" Ringo asked.

"When Shura saved us back in the Emperor domain, she said they would in not so many words. Still, showing up when we were broadcasting to all of Elm... Their timing couldn't have been worse for us."

There was no shortage of exchange students and other Freyjagard citizens staying within Elm's borders. It was foolish to think that the empire wouldn't find out about Yamato's plea to Elm.

Now the Prodigies were forced to make a bitter decision: either side with Yamato and bring discord to their relationship with the empire or refute the call for aid and have the angels themselves renege the Seven Luminaries' guiding philosophy.

"Makes sense why the chick would do that, though. Her showin' up as she did keeps us from sweeping the whole issue under the rug and pretending she was never here. But if you knew they were coming, I take it you've already figured out how you wanna deal with 'em?" Masato questioned.

"That I have." Tsukasa put down his utensils and wiped his mouth. "In fact, that's the very reason I gathered you all here today. As the core members of the Seven Luminaries, I thought it was important that we all get on the same page regarding the situation we now face and the actions we need to take from here on out."

After waiting for everyone to get ready to listen, he cut to the chase.

"Let's start by briefly summarizing the situation. One week ago, we captured a pair of women calling themselves Kaguya and Shura when they invaded our announcement ceremony for the national elections. Then, in accordance with our joint security agreement with Freyjagard, we reported the news to them. When we did, we also asked for their help in identifying the two.

"Three days later, Freyjagard dispatched a diplomat who used to live in Yamato, and with their help, we determined that the women were indeed Kaguya, the first imperial princess of the defeated country of Yamato, and the military leader Shura, who is also known as the White Wolf General. When that fact became clear, the empire informed us that the current Yamato dominion government was demanding they be turned over."

"Yeah, I'll bet." Masato nodded. "Freyjagard can't exactly let royalty from a nation they took over just run around free."

"...What's this about a Yamato dominion government? I was under the impression that Freyjagard had simply annexed them."

Tsukasa gave Keine's question an affirmative dip of his chin. "They did, after Yamato's capital fell and its emperor died, but...Yamato had a fierce resistance movement, and the Freyjagard nobles had little success administrating the country."

As Elch had just mentioned, Yamato didn't have any sort of specialized industries or production. Thus it followed that there were no nobles invested enough in ruling the territory to want to go up against a resistance movement spearheaded by the first imperial princess Kaguya. Despite going to great lengths to invade Yamato, none among the empire's aristocracy actually wanted to hold on to it.

"After a series of trials and tribulations, the empire ultimately returned internal sovereignty to Mayoi, the second imperial princess and a member of the Yamato imperial family who betrayed her homeland and aided Freyjagard during the war, while retaining external sovereignty and ultimate decision-making power over the region. That was how the Yamato dominion settled into the state it's in today."

"Goodness me," Aoi replied. "You mean to say that Kaguya's younger sister was a traitor?"

"I can't speak with any confidence about the way events actually played out, but the public version of accounts certainly seems to suggest as much."

"That's weird, though. If they didn't need it, why bother invading in the first place?" asked Akatsuki.

"...That's an excellent question. It doesn't make sense, and that's something that definitely bears further consideration," Tsukasa replied.

"A-are you sure? I was just kinda curious."

"Absolutely. However, we have more pressing matters to attend to at the moment. We need to consider how we Seven Luminaries are going to respond to the demand made through Freyjagard. Now, I didn't swear any of my staff to silence, so I imagine many of you have already heard, but a few days ago, the official statement I made to the dominion government was—"

Before Tsukasa could go any further, someone interrupted.

"Hey! H-hold on just a minute!"

""".....!""""

Everyone at the meeting heard a loud cry come from outside the dining room.

"Was that Nio just now?" Lyrule inquired.

Tsukasa turned to her and nodded. "It was. Something must have happened."

Nio Harvey was an exchange student from the empire who had come to learn about governing. Tsukasa was the one who'd spent the most time with him, so he rose from his seat to see what was going on.

Yet before he could even finish standing…

"You can't go in there! They're in the middle of a meeting!"

"H-he's right… We can't just rush in out of the blue like this. I—I think we're being hasty…"

"You've got a good head on yer shoulders, Juno, but you always play it too safe! If you wanna get through to 'em, you gotta do it face-to-face!"

""""Yeah, that's right!""""

"The angels said they were here to hear us out, didn't they?! Ain't no reason for us to hold back!"

"L-like I said, if you have something you want to discuss, then as Mr. Tsukasa's secretary, I'm perfectly equipped to pass on a message…"

"We wanna talk to the angels in person! 'Sides, you're one of them imperial exchange students, aren'tcha? This is an Elm issue, so keep your nose out of it!"

"But I— Ah!"

"Excuse us; comin' through!"

The dining room door swung open with a bang, and eight brawny men wearing grubby outfits noisily barged in.

Masato reacted to the unexpected newcomers by casting a snide look Tsukasa's way. "Whoa, you double-booked the room? That's not a great look, Prime Minister Mikogami."

"They aren't here by appointment. It's not my fault." After replying to Masato's dig, Tsukasa looked to Nio, who had followed the men in. "Nio?"

"I-I'm terribly sorry. I told them that you were in the middle of a meeting and that they needed to come back later, but..."

"That's fine. More importantly, who are they?"

Instead of Nio, however, Tsukasa found his question answered by the large, bull-horned *byuma* heading up the group's vanguard.

"Our bad for chargin' in uninvited! Er, I mean, we're sorry? No, no... 'Our humblest apologies'! We're a group of humble farmers from Narnia, in the Buchwald domain, and we're here today 'cause our leader's got something she needs to tell y'all angels!"

The men made no attempts to hide their identities, and between the dirt under their nails, the stained state of their clothes, and the calluses on their hands, a single glance was enough for Tsukasa to tell that they were precisely who they claimed to be. Furthermore, that none of them were armed informed him that they truly did just wish to speak.

As such—

"I'm Tsukasa, the angel entrusted by God Akatsuki in matters of state. If you have something to say, I'll hear you out."

—he gave Aoi, who had been readying herself to suppress the

intruders, a look to tell her she could stand down. Then, he turned to the men and gave them his full attention.

"C'mon, Juno! Yer up!" responded the large *byuma*, and he gave the young woman hiding behind him a little push. She was short, wearing glasses, and looked to be about twenty.

"I—I can't. This is all so sudden; m-my heart isn't ready yet…"

"You've been goin' on about this since yesterday, haven't ya?! You're a smart cookie, so have some confidence!"

"Eeep!"

The man gave the bespectacled woman a solid clap on the back, and she stumbled all the way up to Tsukasa. If the horned man was having her take over, then she must have been the aforementioned leader.

Tsukasa's eyes fell upon Juno. Realizing that it was too late to back out, she stopped glancing around nervously and timidly began her speech.

"…My, um, my name is Juno, and I'm Narnia City's treasurer. First of all, I'd like to apologize again for barging in on you in the middle of a meal. I'm so sorry."

"Think nothing of it. As angels, listening to what the people have to say is our foremost priority… Isn't that right, God Akatsuki?"

"Huh?! Oh yeah! Totally! Verily, I mean! Bwa-ha-ha-ha!"

"You have our deepest thanks for your magnanimity, God Akatsuki," said Juno with a bow of her head.

"So what is it you came here to tell us?" Tsukasa pressed.

"Be-before that, I have a question I'd like to ask. If it turns out that what we heard wasn't true, then it would mean that all my fears are baseless."

"Oh? And what is it you heard?"

Juno met Tsukasa's gaze as she posed her inquiry. "There's a rumor going around that the Seven Luminaries have rejected the empire's demand that we extradite Princess Kaguya of Yamato, the woman who crashed the election announcement the other day. Is this true?"

"_____"

Ironically enough, Juno's question was getting at the same thing Tsukasa was going to tell the others about before they were so rudely interrupted.

Everyone wanted to know how he had replied to the dominion government's insistence that Kaguya be relinquished into its custody.

Tsukasa gave his answer plainly.

"It is. As the angel entrusted by God Akatsuki with matters of state, I personally informed the dominion government via Freyjagard that both Kaguya and Shura are criminals being held for the offense of illegal entry into the Republic of Elm, and we're unable to deport them until after they've served their sentences."

"""""Wh—?!"""""

"What in tarnation wouldja do that for?!"

The moment they heard Tsukasa's reply, the farmers' expressions froze with panic, and Juno was thrown for such a loop that she lapsed back into her rustic accent.

When she realized her mistake, her face went bright red, but after clearing her throat to regain her composure, she stared at Tsukasa with renewed determination.

"The two of them are wanted in the empire for high crimes. One of them is the *princess of Yamato*. And what's more, the whole nation knows that they asked the Seven Luminaries for help liberating their home. Doubtless, Freyjagard must know of this as well. In light of all that, I don't comprehend how your decision is anything other than sheltering felons from the empire! I beg of you, please accept Freyjagard's demand and extradite the Yamato princess! I see no good reason why we should have to take on such risk for the sake of a nation that hasn't existed for years!"

"And that's what you're here about?" Tsukasa questioned.

"You'd better believe it!" one of the farmers replied. "Ever since Juno heard 'bout the rumor, she's been saying that we might piss off the empire and start another war! That's why we all came over to ask y'all to change your minds! Ain't that right, Juno?!"

"I-it is… When I first heard what you did, my immediate thought was that beings as exalted as you all might not understand the animosity you risked breeding in the empire by refusing their demand. Unlike you, we humans are petty and narrow-minded.

"You can assert that your decision is based on accords made between Elm and Freyjagard, but there's no guarantee there won't be people who get enraged regardless and turn to violence to get their way. I implore you, turn the two women over as soon as possible. We don't want our peace destroyed!"

"I see." Tsukasa was impressed by Juno's earnest plea. She had seen the diplomatic implications of their situation with stellar clarity.

And she was right—even though Tsukasa was acting per the joint security agreement, his refusal to deport Kaguya would no doubt inspire unjust anger in the empire all the same.

Furthermore, choosing to take such a hard-line, by-the-book attitude with a party they had only just signed a cease-fire treaty with could hardly be described as tactful.

However…Tsukasa already knew all that. He'd made his choice despite it. And he had had good cause for doing so.

As such—

"I appreciate you coming to me with your concerns. Yet I'm afraid I can't do that."

—he curtly shot her down.

"B-but… But why?!"

"There are two reasons. The first is that when an individual commits a crime in a foreign nation, they're only to be forcefully repatriated after they've been punished by local law. That was what we and the empire decided in the joint security agreement we made after the cease-fire. Unless they can convince us otherwise, I see no justification for making an exception of those two solely for the sake of Freyjagard's convenience. The second reason is that we act per the ideal of equality for all. As such, we can't dismiss Kaguya's plea to save Yamato without at least affording it due consideration."

"Hey, whoa, hold up!" one of the farmers interjected. "You mean you're just gonna believe that princess chick outta nowhere and back Yamato?!"

"If what she says is true, and her people do need our aid, then it's in keeping with our principles that the Seven Luminaries, and in turn the Republic of Elm, convince the empire to correct whatever injustices are being perpetrated."

"But if ya do that, it'd mean war!"

"Yeah! It's too dangerous!"

Tsukasa answered the pale-faced farmers with a stern tone. "It won't come to that. The empire is a valuable partner to us, and I have the *utmost confidence* that our relationship with them will hold strong for a long while to come."

"You talk real slippery-like, don'tcha...?" Juno grumbled quietly.

"I wouldn't be doing my job as a politician if I didn't."

Juno's accusation had an almost disappointed ring to it, and Tsukasa replied as shamelessly as could be.

Even if, hypothetically, he was considering making Freyjagard listen by force if they refused his demand, as a part of Elm's government, he would never dream of saying so out loud.

However—

"That said...while we have every intention of approaching this issue via economic aid and diplomatic efforts, if the empire responds to us with hostility, I don't deny the possibility that we'll have to reply in kind."

—he was willing to admit the chance of Freyjagard forcing Elm's hand.

By doing so, Tsukasa was indirectly communicating to Juno and her entourage that their fear about him and the other angels not understanding the subtleties of human emotion was unfounded. This revealed that the Seven Luminaries chose not to extradite Kaguya knowing it might lead to war, while also affirming that Tsukasa's political stance was that equality for all was more important than Elm's relationship with Freyjagard.

"…Is…that so…?"

Juno let out a long exhale and closed her eyes. She was steeling herself. After a few seconds of silence, she opened her eyes, narrowed them, looked at Tsukasa and the other five Prodigies, and spoke with a voice positively brimming with animosity.

"I get it now. There ain't no point in trusting you."

"What makes you say that?" asked Tsukasa.

"All them things you said were moving and true. But they're all just platitudes. God Akatsuki showed us that you angels can survive being cut in two, but we humans aren't like that. If we die, that's the end for us. And that means we can't afford to put our lives on the line for niceties. We can't go marching off to our deaths for the sake of your lofty ideals. So if you all would have us die to uphold them…then we the people have no choice but to rise against you to protect ourselves."

No sooner did Juno finish her impassioned speech—

"I refuse to stand idly by and listen to this!"

""""———?!"""""

—than a new voice cut through the chamber, and the doors on the far side from where Juno and the farmers had entered swung violently open.

Eight burly men and a silvery-haired woman dressed in red appeared. Immediately, the woman shouted at Juno and the farmers in a tone shaking with fury.

"Not only do you object to divine providence, but you even have the nerve to threaten the angels?!"

"…Today's quite the day for unannounced visitors, I see."

Tsukasa gave a light shrug, then directed an inquisitive glance at the new guests.

The ash-blond-haired *hyuma* woman who looked to be the group's leader gave him a deep bow.

"I beg your pardon for our sudden entrance, Mr. Angel. I am Tetra, captain of the Vigilante Corps that serves Hamel and fifteen other villages in the Gustav domain! And the men behind me are members of that corps!"

""""Pardon the intrusion, sir!""""

"Oh…! That would make you Great Scythe Tetra, then?"

When the woman introduced herself while inclining at a sharp ninety-degree angle, Tsukasa recalled having heard her name before.

Gustav's region during his rule had been a breeding ground for poverty and lawlessness. But as the story went, a single brave woman organized a large-scale vigilante group to protect the area's villages and also stood on the front lines herself and mowed down bandits with a massive scythe.

If Tsukasa recalled correctly, that hero's name had indeed been Tetra.

Tetra herself confirmed his suspicions. "For the name of one such as I to have reached your exalted ears…it's a great honor, sir!"

Merely standing across from her was enough to make Tsukasa's skin bristle with tension.

Aoi was also far more on guard than she had been when Juno's group entered. Thus, there was little reason not to believe the red-garbed woman's claims.

"We came here today to report something to you, but while we had every intention of waiting outside the room until you finished your current appointment…when I overheard the blasphemy coming from inside, I couldn't bear to remain silent. I ask that you forgive my impropriety."

"…I see. Well, that's all well and good, but are you planning on raising your head at some point?"

After first bowing, Tetra had yet to stop. She gave her reply while her face was still pointed directly at the ground.

"N-no sir! I would never dream of being so irreverent as to lift my head to the same level as an angel's!"

"…Your piety is impressive." It may have been for the greater good, but as one of the people deceiving her, Tsukasa still felt a pang of guilt. "However, I can't say I'm too fond of staring at someone's scalp while I talk to them. Would you mind looking at me?"

"F-forgive me! Th-then by your leave, I shall raise my gaze alone." With that, Tetra turned her face up toward Tsukasa while leaving her back bent. Her expression was the very image of sincerity.

…If not for that earnestness, it would have felt like she was mocking him.

Tsukasa shot a stern look at Masato to stop him from bursting into laughter, then spoke.

"I see. Then as an angel of the Seven Luminaries, I order you thus—stop bowing and straighten up normally."

"A-as you wish!"

After being given a direct order by an angel, Tetra finally relented. Now that they were at last at eye level, Tsukasa could get on with business.

"So what was it you came here to tell us?"

"Sir! With all due respect, in the week since the Yamato princess came seeking our aid, you angels have yet to begin amassing troops. Upon noticing that, I couldn't help but fear you were acting out of consideration for the residents of Elm, so I felt it was my duty to come convey the will of the people to you!"

"And what might that be?"

"Sir! We wish to abide by the Seven Luminaries' glorious philosophy of equality for all and rescue Yamato without a moment's hesitation! No, not just Yamato—we would deliver salvation to every nation in the world whose people suffer under the yoke of oppression. It was the principle of equality for all that gave rise to our great Republic, and I see it as our responsibility to spread that ideology across the globe! Thus, Elm has a duty to fight for the sake of that ideal. Hoarding the liberation we've been afforded would be utterly inexcusable. And yet..."

Tetra paused to stare at Juno's group as harshly as when she had first barged in.

"...You people! Are you truly base enough to abandon Yamato to its fate despite recently having been saved by the angels' grace yourselves?! Selfish cowards, the lot of you! The angels are trying to bring deliverance to us per their sublime goal. If saving Yamato means war, then that struggle would be no less than a holy endeavor! As people rescued by the angels, we should be honored to take part in such an undertaking!"

The large men behind Tetra followed her sermon by yelling at Juno and the farmers.

"Yeah! Tetra's right!"

"What, you think everyone else can go suck it as long as you've got yours?!"

Juno shrank back at their angry cries, but her allies weren't so easily cowed.

"The hell you people talkin' about?! Why should we put ourselves on the line for a bunch of foreigners?!"

"Yeah! A government's gotta look out for its own citizens before it starts worryin' about a bunch of people off somewhere else!"

"And whenever there's a war, it's always us little guys you collect tons of taxes from! If y'all love fighting so much, then go take your bloodthirsty angels and battle it on your own!"

The farmers met Tetra's group's criticism by shouting back that they were in the right.

"The masses don't want war," they cried.

"No, the people will join our holy crusade with joy," the other side shouted back.

The air was rife with voices championing rival ideologies. Each exchange grew more and more heated, and before long—

"Insulting us is one thing, but calling the angels bloodthirsty…?! This affront cannot stand! Perhaps you need someone to beat your rotten hearts into shape!"

"Ha! I'd like to see y'all try!"

—the two factions were on the verge of coming to blows.

Fortunately, Aoi reacted quickly to the mounting tension.

Knowing she needed to put a lid on the situation, she drew her blade.

"EVERYONE, QUIET!!!!"

"""""" .... """"""

Yet before the swordfighter could do anything, Tsukasa's voice

Sacraneco

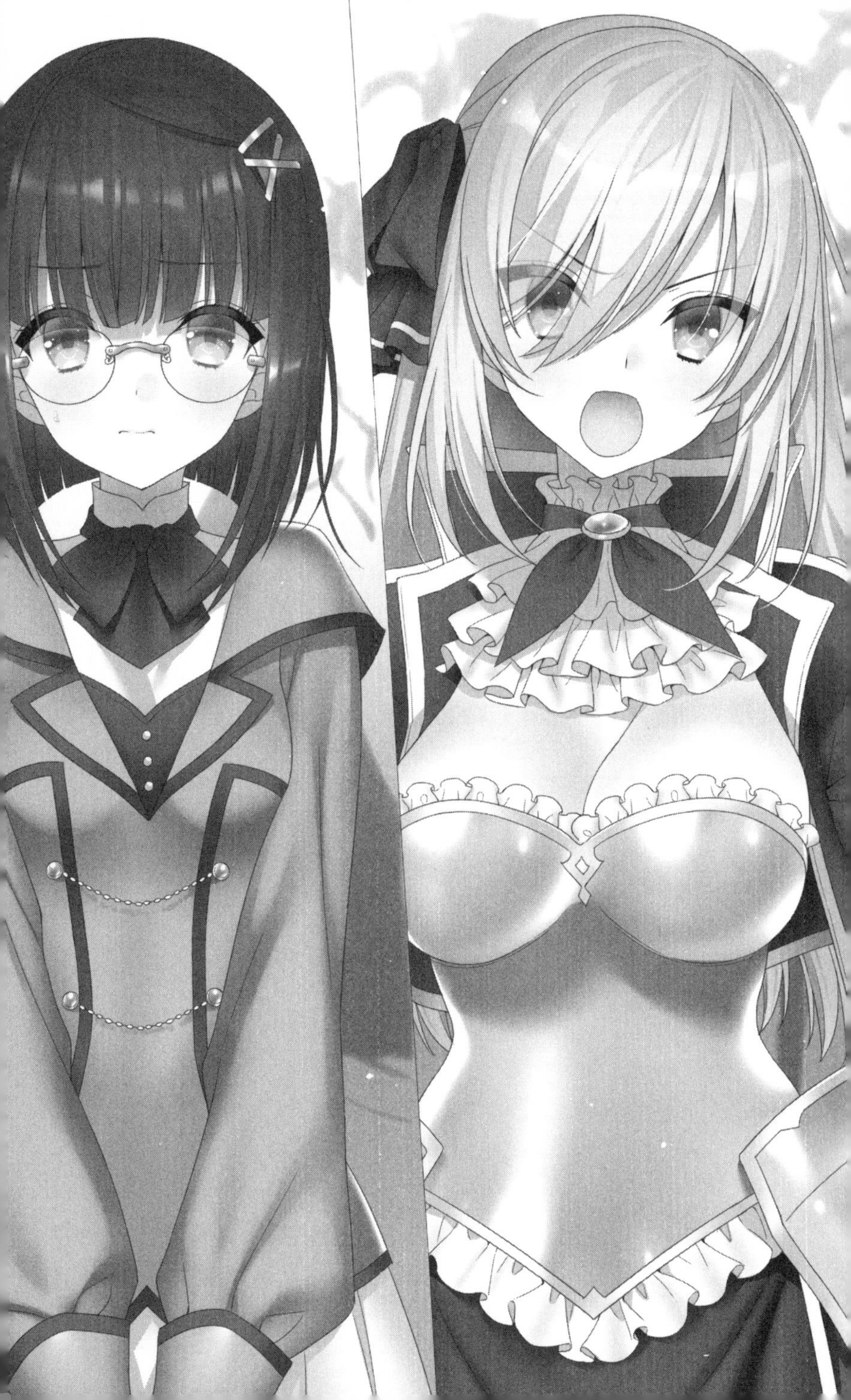

boomed a thunderclap. Even the windows shook. Few, if any, of their visitors had expected such a roar to come from a man as slight as Tsukasa. Tetra and the others froze in shock.

Tsukasa swept his gaze across them as he spoke. "I can see that everyone feels strongly about how the Yamato situation should be handled. However, altogether you are only eighteen people, and there's no way to draw meaningful conclusions about the populace's opinion from such a small sample. If you want to find out where the consensus lies, the only way to do so is by asking every person in the Republic of Elm. And it just so happens…that we've already prepared a stage for doing exactly that. Isn't that right, Juno?"

The woman gave him just the reply he was looking for.

"…You mean the national elections."

"I do indeed. There's no restriction that says those who disagree with the Seven Luminaries' way of doing things can't run. The candidates are free to choose their platforms however they see fit, and the people are free to vote as they please. That's how democracies like Elm work. Instead of wasting your breath shouting over one another in this tiny room, I think you'd be better served by going out recruiting like-minded allies for the election. If your opinions truly reflect the majority's will, you should expect to see that reflected in the vote. Isn't that right, Tetra?"

Tetra straightened her back and apologized.

"Sir! Absolutely, sir! I'm terribly sorry for losing my temper and putting on this unseemly display!"

Hearing that made her realize that justice was on her side. The masses would never agree to besmirch the wonderful ideal of equality by pandering to the empire and forsaking Yamato. Once it was time to vote, the selfish fools before her would find their upstart notions rejected. And once that happened, the cowards would have to realize the error of their ways.

"Now, I'd like to ask you all to leave. We still have matters we need to discuss among ourselves."

Now that both sides had calmed down, Tsukasa called for them to disperse. His bellow from earlier had left quite an impression.

Instead of quarreling any further, the two women and the men behind them bowed and left the same way they had come in.

Once the doors on both sides clicked shut—

"Wh-wh-what the heck?! What just happened?!"

—Akatsuki immediately went pale as a sheet.

"Th-the second group was one thing, but the first one said they were gonna rise up against us! Isn't that, like, treason?! Like, a mutiny?! Wh-wh-wh-wh-what do we do?! Crush them? Crush them, right?!"

"Geez, Prince, dial it back a notch."

"Masato is right, that he is. There were scarcely more than a handful of them, and I could have managed the situation with ease. Worry not and keep your dignity about you, m'lord," Aoi assured.

However, Elch remained unconvinced. "…Just a handful for now, maybe."

"Elch, m'lord? What do you mean by that?"

"Ever since those two crashed the election announcement, more and more people have been getting worried that our treaty with the empire won't last. It's worsening every day, and I've heard that public opinion of the Seven Luminaries' government is starting to take a turn for the worse."

Folks were frightened that they might get dragged into another war with the empire if they kept following the Seven Luminaries.

Juno's group may have been the only one who came to express as much in person, but that didn't mean they were the only party who felt that way.

Fear and distrust were building, and there was no release valve in sight.

Elch worked more closely with the general populace than the High School Prodigies did. He could sense the shifting opinions all the more keenly.

With the war for liberation over, the nation was starting to lose its unity.

Elch felt obligated to offer a suggestion to Tsukasa, the nation's secretary of the interior.

"Shouldn't we start taking steps to prevent an insurrection?"

Yet Tsukasa shook his head.

"That won't be necessary."

"B-but, Tsukasa! Those guys said they were gonna rise up!" Akatsuki yelped.

"When they said that, they weren't talking about armed rebellion. That Juno woman is wiser than she looks. She chose her words carefully, knowing that, as angels preaching salvation, we can't take heavy-handed measures against people for merely defending themselves. She saw us take the empire's four northern domains in a few short months, so she understands the power differential she's up against. No…when she declared she would rise up against us, she was alluding to winning the people over in the election and delivering a vote of no confidence against the Seven Luminaries."

Proof of that could be found in the fact that Juno understood just what sort of function an election served. There was no reason to crack down on what she was doing.

As Tsukasa laid out his stance—

"Tsukasa…?"

—Lyrule gave him a perplexed look from the seat beside him.

When Tsukasa realized that, he tilted his head to the side.

"Hmm? What is it, Lyrule?"

"Oh, nothing. It's just…you looked like you were *having fun*."

Tsukasa realized that a faint smile was playing on his lips. His emotions had started creeping onto his face without him even noticing it. That said, he had no particular reason to hide it.

"Having fun? Yes, I suppose I was. This is something to be celebrated."

"I-it is? Even with things about to come to a head like they are?"

"Not long ago, those men and women would have left themselves at the whim of the tides, even if the ship that was their nation was heading toward the great waterfall called war. But they've changed. Both Juno's group, who believes that a country should prioritize its welfare above all else, and Tetra's group, who disagrees and feels that we should save Yamato in keeping with the Seven Luminaries' principles, have clear visions for what direction they want the country to go in and are taking the initiative to try to steer the ship that way."

In other words, the idea that the people should choose their nation's trajectory was starting to take root in the populace. Democracy didn't work unless all believed that they were their own masters. However, that was a hard thing for those at the bottom of the world's ruling structure to buy into.

To them, a country was a ship controlled by the privileged, and they were merely slaves being made to row. They had no right to choose its heading. The very thought was ludicrous. Yet now, thanks to their belief in the doctrine of equality for all and their newfound independence from the empire, their attitudes were slowly beginning to shift. Juno's and Tetra's visits were only the beginning.

"This marks a monumental step forward for the Republic of Elm," declared Tsukasa.

Winona nodded from her seat beside Elch's. "Yeah, definitely feels like people are changin' a bit. Hell, even just the fact that they're complaining 'bout their worries and grievances woulda been unthinkable back when the empire was in charge… By the way, Tsukasa, which of those two you think has it right?"

"I…don't believe that anything as simple as 'correct' or 'incorrect' exists in the world of politics. For instance, a king's job is to make their land prosperous, but that sometimes means having to suck wealth out of other countries, and doing so will draw criticism. However, if the king decides to prioritize fostering strong foreign relationships, then they'll be criticized in turn for not doing enough to help their people. Politics is all about making trade-offs, and being a politician isn't about finding the 'best' solution—it's about finding the 'better' one."

The best outcome for Group A might very well be the worst for Group B.

"Comparing their opinions with that in mind, though… I would say that Tetra's way of thinking is closer to the 'better' solution."

"It…is…?" Ringo found that surprising. She was a timid person by nature, so to her, Tetra's belligerent opinion had come across as almost scary.

"Comparatively speaking, yes," Tsukasa replied. "While I won't deny that Tetra's philosophy is dangerously aggressive, Juno's is actually the more dangerous of the two. The idea that we can preserve the peace by handing Kaguya and Shura over to the empire is deeply misguided. In fact, it would do the exact opposite. Handing them over would only serve to damage the most crucial element toward maintaining peace… Nio?"

"Y-yes?!"

"Why do you think wars happen?"

"Um…"

Tsukasa's sudden question gave Nio, who had missed his opportunity to leave the room, a bit of pause. After a moment, he gave his answer.

"There can be historical issues or economic factors, and sometimes troops are also dispatched for domestic reasons like wanting to weaken lesser lords' forces. There are usually a lot of factors and motives at play, so it's hard to speak unilaterally."

However, Tsukasa shook his head.

"It's not hard at all. You see, Nio, all the things you just listed off are nothing more than pretexts. The heart of the issue is something much simpler. Maybe I should ask it a different way. Let's suppose you were utterly destitute, and you hadn't eaten anything in a week. However, your neighbors were affluent and had gold and food to spare. Under those circumstances, would you steal from your neighbor's house?"

"O-of course not! I would never stoop so low!"

"You're a good kid, Nio."

"Huh?!"

As Nio's cheeks turned bright red, Tsukasa went on.

"However, the only reason you say that is because you're well educated and have a sound character.

"Not everyone is like you. There are people in this world lacking in morals who don't think twice about violently seizing things from others. You could say that your neighbors in the hypothetical were immoral for letting you starve and not sharing their surplus food with you themselves. And the same holds just as true for nations as it does for individuals. The reason war happens is that people with flawed characters and no sympathy for others attain positions of power."

If both sides were good and just, then the one in poverty wouldn't steal, and the one with wealth would share it freely. Peace would reign throughout the world. But when a faction—or both—lacked a good conscience, then that didn't happen.

"This world suffers from a stark shortage of ethics. That was true of many of the nobles we fought, and there are still plenty of influentials who view commoners as nothing more than pets or objects. They don't think of them as human, so they don't hesitate to take from them as they please. And when that's the way they treat their own country-men, it goes without saying that they don't lose a wink of sleep over what befalls poorer folks in other nations."

In this world, the strong only recognized the humanity of the strong. Commoners were like stalks of wheat growing from the ground to the aristocracy, and they mowed them down without a second thought.

"But that's unsustainable. Any castle built on a rotting founda-tion will soon crumble, no matter how strong it is," Tsukasa stated. "We could do as Juno's group said and make friendly with the empire, yes, but it wouldn't bring about the era of peace that they're looking for. To achieve true harmony, the ideology of equality for all can't stop at Elm's borders. It needs to become an internationally recognized standard.

"People seek out labels, like *commoner* and *enemy country*, as an excuse to hurt others. It's imperative that we foster a more moral world that acknowledges that doing so is evil and denounces such things as evil."

Back in the Prodigies' world, global weariness about war caused by a pair of nationalism-driven world conflicts had led to an unprec-edented push for ethical systems that transcended national borders. Once these policies spread, it created a global environment where even nations with overwhelming military might could no longer thought-lessly wield their power. It wasn't a perfect solution by any stretch of the imagination. Still, the difference between Earth and this planet was like night and day.

War was kept in check through morality, not force. Humans were the only animals who could claim to have achieved that feat in all the Earth's history. It was an advancement on par with the discovery of fire. Now the planet the Prodigies inhabited was in need of the same ethical development and diffusion.

"As such, we can't write the Yamato situation off as a mere issue for Freyjagard to handle internally. It's common courtesy to stay out of other nations' domestic affairs, but that doesn't mean courtesy can be prioritized over basic human rights. Even if it's happening in another country, that doesn't change the fact that wrong is wrong. As proponents of equality for all, we must do everything in our power to correct the situation, both for its own sake and as an example for generations to come. Now, as far as our plan for the immediate future goes…"

With that, Tsukasa continued from where he had left off before Juno and the others had interrupted him.

"For the most part, our plans for the election remain unchanged. As we hand over the reins of power, though, we should investigate whether Yamato actually needs the help that Kaguya claims it does. If so, we'll need to prepare to make firm demands that the empire rectify the situation. Furthermore, we should keep in mind that the empire is unlikely to cooperate readily. We have a lot of work ahead of us that I didn't initially account for, so…I hope I can continue depending on you all."

"I have no objections," Keine replied.

"Nor I. My blade is yours, that it is," Aoi chimed in.

"W-well, if you say it's important…," Akatsuki said.

"I'll do…my best…," Ringo agreed.

Tsukasa's allies nodded in agreement.

Their dear friends lived in this world, and they wanted to build an era of peace and stability for them. It was a sentiment shared by all seven of the high schoolers, the absent Shinobu Sarutobi included. None had a reason to begrudge the legwork Tsukasa's plans would necessitate.

Yet—

"Count me opposed."

—one member of the group, Prodigy businessman Masato Sanada, voiced his dissent.

"Huh…?" Akatsuki froze when he heard Masato's objection. It wasn't just the Prodigy magician, either. Everyone present stared at Masato in wordless shock.

"M-Masato…? What was that you just said…?"

"Clean out your ears, man. I said I'm opposed." After answering Akatsuki by restating his objection to the proposal, Masato began tapping his teaspoon against the rim of his teacup in annoyance as he glared at Tsukasa. "I mean, Tsukasa, are you even hearin' yourself right now? In case you forgot, *that grandmaster's our only way of getting back to Earth.* The hell you gonna do if we piss him off?"

Lyrule and Elch raised their voices in alarm.

"M-Masato?!"

"Hey, man, watch what you say! And *where* you say it!"

Everyone else stared at the businessman in disbelief as well, but none so much as Nio.

"Huh? The grandmaster…?"

Someday, the High School Prodigies were going to go back home to Earth. They had their own lives to return to, after all. That was why they had set up their Seven Luminaries teachings. The hope was that they could hand power over to the native populace smoothly and depart.

However, they had deliberately kept it a secret that their current

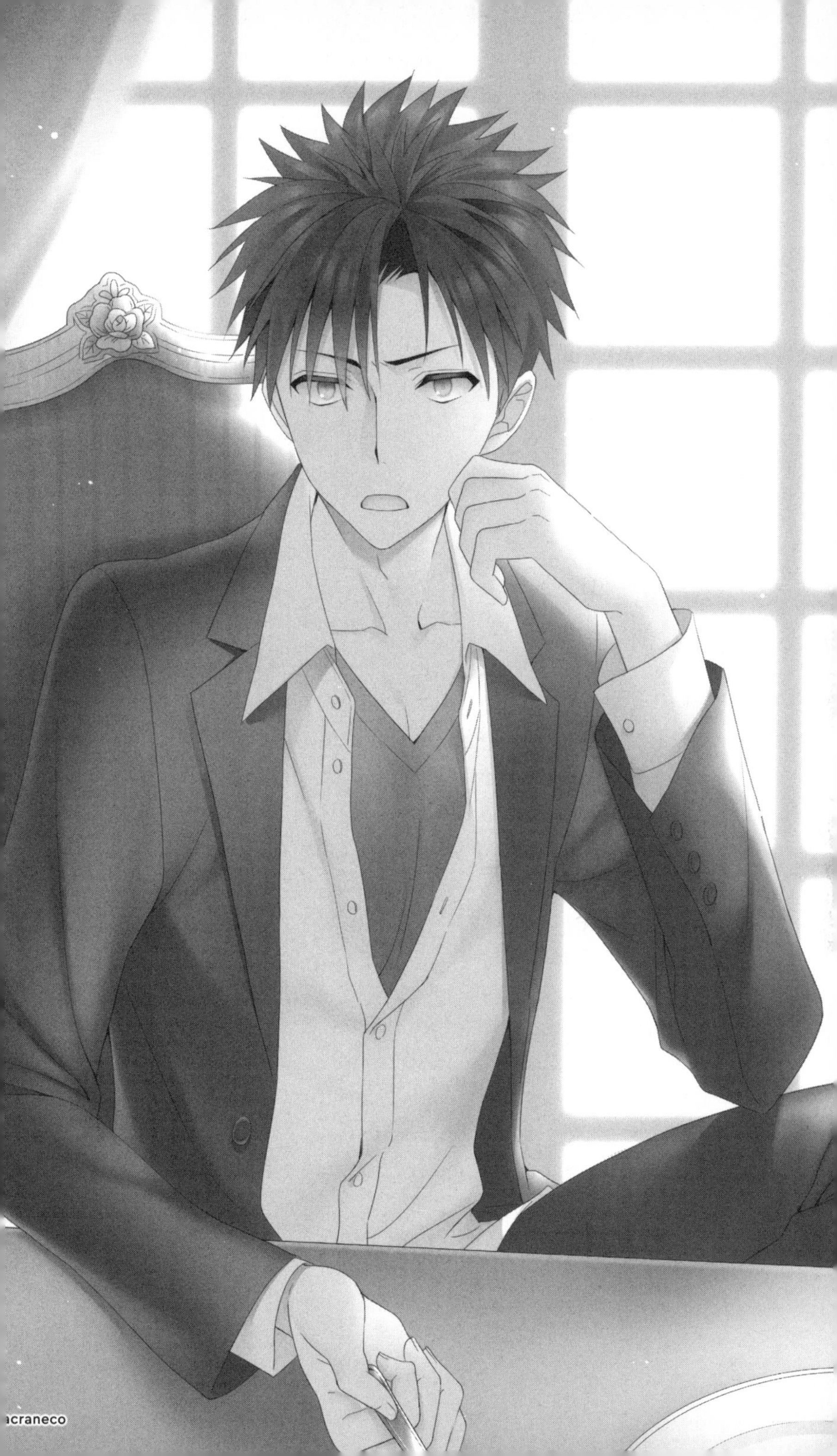
acraneco

method for getting home involved the aid of Imperial Grandmaster Neuro. Not only would that fact call their divinity into question, but it would also raise concerns about whether they could be trusted at all.

And yet Masato had now revealed it not just to an outsider, but to Nio, an exchange student from the empire.

It was a blunder that couldn't be undone.

Upon seeing everyone's faces, Nio realized he had heard something he shouldn't have.

"It, um, it sounds like you all have something important to talk about! I'll just see myself out!"

Thus, he hurriedly tried to scamper out of the room.

"No, it's fine. Stay. I'll explain it all later." Tsukasa stopped him in his tracks, however.

The damage was already done. Now the only option was to explain the situation and ask that Nio keep his silence.

Letting him wander off to who knows where with the knowledge he now had would be far more dangerous.

"That was careless, Merchant."

"You wanna talk about careless? You're the one pickin' a fight with the grandmaster." Not fazed in the slightest by Tsukasa's rebuke, Masato put down the teaspoon he'd been restlessly tapping his cup with and downed his tea in a single gulp. The brusque manner in which he did so made it all too clear how annoyed the young man was.

"Your concern is valid, Merchant. But cultivating a worldwide system of moral beliefs founded in humanism is essential for maintaining international peace; you know that."

"Yeah, sure, that's all fine and dandy. What I'm sayin' is that we've got no reason to put our one ticket home in danger just to develop all that."

"It may have been a means to an end, but the fact remains that we were the ones who built a nation here founded on the belief of equality for *all*, not just those with distinguished families and noble bloodlines. We accelerated what would normally have taken these people hundreds of years to develop on their own. And because of that, we have a duty to ensure that it finds its legs.

"If we turned down Princess Kaguya's plea solely to protect our relationship with Grandmaster Neuro, then we would be leaving a black mark on this world's history and deny humanism the chance to reach global acceptance. That would be a depraved act of selfishness on our part, would it not?"

"And what's so wrong with that?"

"……!" Tsukasa gasped at Masato's curt response.

"Nothing, that's what. This world ain't the only thing we've got a responsibility toward, y'know. I've got people who count on me. I'm talking about my company. My *employees*. I have an obligation to them. I'm mad grateful to Lyrule and Winona, don't get me wrong, but you compare what I owe this planet to that obligation, and the two aren't even close."

Masato rose from his chair as he spoke.

"Honestly, the grandmaster's sketchy as hell. I get why you're wary of him; I do. And there was that whole bit about the world being in crisis, too. But at the end of the day, *I believe he's telling the truth when he says he'll send us home*. So if you're over here talkin' about potentially getting on his bad side, then it means you and I are after different things. So from here on, you can count me out."

Masato was talking about parting ways.

Akatsuki let out a cry that was practically a scream. "M-Masato, you're kidding, right…?!"

Yet astonishingly—

"Very well."

—their resolute leader, Tsukasa, accepted Masato's divisive statement without pause.

"Tsukasa?! Wh-what do you mean, 'very well'?!" Akatsuki cried, gaping in disbelief.

"The reason we agreed to work together in the first place was that we recognized it would let us search more efficiently for a way to get back to Earth. But Merchant is right. Strictly from the perspective of wanting to get home, the decision I'm making can hardly be described as apt. Thus…I have no reason to stop him."

"B-but still…"

"I have to ask, though, Merchant, what specifically do you mean when you say you want out? Grandmaster Neuro may know about our situation, but if you stay in Elm, I find it hard to imagine him believing that you've actually cut ties with us. Even if it's just temporary, you'll probably need to put some distance between us. Do you have an idea of where you plan to go?"

Despite Akatsuki's continued opposition, Tsukasa shifted his gaze back to Masato, who replied without hesitation.

"The vice chief of the Lakan Archipelago Alliance is tryin' to poach me. I'm gonna head her way for a while."

"I see… In that case, we can announce that the Seven Luminaries will be dispatching one of its angels to Lakan to proselytize equality for all. We can't afford to have our internal disunity become public, not when we haven't even handed over power yet."

"Yeah, I'll make sure to keep up the cover. It's not like I'm tryin' to screw you guys. But just know that if you botch things with the grandmaster bad enough to start a war, I'm telling the world how I seceded from the Seven Luminaries." Masato was drawing a line in the sand—ticking off Neuro was the one thing he wouldn't do.

Tsukasa respected his friend's conviction. "Of course. That's perfectly fair," he replied. "You've been a tremendous help up until now. On behalf of everyone, I'd like to thank you for everything."

A lonely smile spread across the young prime minister's face. That was his way of saying he wouldn't try to change Masato's mind, even if it meant losing a friend.

"...Yeah." Masato accepted Tsukasa's gratitude and turned around.

"Hey, what?! Wait, Masato, hold up! I— Ow!"

Ignoring Akatsuki, who had banged his knee on the table in his haste to try to stop him, Masato left the room alone. The double doors slammed shut behind him. The whole turn of events was so sudden that Akatsuki forgot all about Nio and rushed over to Tsukasa.

"You're really just gonna let him go like that?!"

Even Winona, who had watched everything unfold, felt the need to speak up. "Tsukasa, we all appreciate everything you've done for us. But nobody's asking you to keep looking after us if it costs you your friendships."

Elch and Lyrule nodded in agreement. Still, Tsukasa shook his head.

"I know. However, regardless of how we got here, the fact remains that we were the ones who accelerated your world's culture. We guided the People's Revolution to success and founded a democracy with no regard for the proper process those things were supposed to take.

"As such, I hold that our foremost priority should be making sure that this nation is strong enough to weather the coming transition to a more enlightened era. That's something I'm not going to back down on. I'm not doing this for the sake of this world—it's for my own pride and dignity."

Tsukasa was determined to take responsibility for what he'd said and done. There was no abandoning things midway through. To the young prime minister, doing so was the greatest sin a politician could commit.

Lawmakers were people who earned trust from others through their promises. In Tsukasa's eyes, anyone who weaseled their way out of those commitments and pushed their responsibilities off onto others was no politician at all. They were nothing but a parasite leeching off their country.

Even though Tsukasa wasn't in Japan, and none of his voters were there to keep him accountable, his pride and dignity denied him any corner cutting. That fastidious pursuit of virtue was what had earned him the moniker of Prodigy politician in the first place.

"…That said, the fact that we've met someone who can get us home means that the circumstances we first formed this alliance under have changed. Now would be a good time for the rest of you all to reconsider how you want to proceed. If you disagree with the direction I'm taking, I won't ask that you force yourselves to accompany me. Just as Merchant stated, the decision I'm making endangers our relationship with Grandmaster Neuro and carries considerable risk for us."

"I intend to continue collaborating with you, just as I have." The first reply came from Keine, who didn't show a moment's hesitation.

"While I would certainly prefer to avoid drawing the grandmaster's ire, my long history on the battlefield has taught me *precisely* how important the morals you espouse are. And what's more, if negotiations break down, and the Yamato situation devolves into war, then I daresay I'll have my work cut out for me."

Aoi followed her lead. "I shall follow you as well, m'lord. If battle comes, my skills may be of some use… And I have personal business with Yamato as well, that I do."

"Finding a replacement for Hoozukimaru, you mean?"

Aoi gave Tsukasa's sharp remark a nod.

"Verily. If we get involved with Yamato, we may cross paths with the one who forged those two's blades. Returning to Earth empty-handed would impede my future endeavors, that it would."

"Fair enough. I'll make sure to ask Shura if she knows anything."

"You have my thanks."

After Aoi, Ringo chimed in.

"…I'm…with you…too, Tsukasa. There's still…a lot of things…I still need to do…here." She, too, was prepared to continue working for Elm's sake under Tsukasa's leadership.

"Thank you, Ringo. That means a lot."

That left only Akatsuki.

"I—I…"

Inevitably, everyone else turned toward him.

Now that he was the center of attention—

"_____!"

—he leaped up as though unable to endure their gazes and rushed out of the room.

After fleeing, Akatsuki glanced around, looking for Masato.

Eventually, he spotted him down the hallway. The Prodigy businessman hadn't stopped or looked back once. The distance he'd covered was evidence of that, and Akatsuki felt a twinge of pain in his heart.

Masato was serious about this. This wasn't some prank he was pulling. The young man indeed was planning on parting ways with them here.

Technically, Tsukasa was right. The reason the Prodigies had joined forces was so they could get back home. It made complete sense that they'd split up if their goals fell out of alignment. Everything about it was perfectly logical. Yet in Akatsuki's mind, crash-landing on this alien world had made the seven teenagers into inseparable comrades. To him, the idea of their scattering to the winds was unthinkable.

He hated it. The thought of the group splitting up was terrifying. Spurred on by that terror, Akatsuki called out to his departing friend.

"MASATOOO!"

It was the loudest voice his throat could muster. Masato's shoulders twitched at the unexpected bellow—

"Hwah?! G-geez, you gave me a heart attack! What's with the shouting, Prince?"

—then he stopped in his tracks and turned toward Akatsuki.

"'What's with the shouting'? How could I not after you said all that dumb stuff...?!"

Akatsuki ran up to Masato, chewed him out—

"C'mon, man, let's go back. You and me, together. I don't want us to get all split up..."

—then tugged on his sleeve and asked him to reconsider. His tone was almost pleading.

Masato took one look at Akatsuki's pathetic expression and laughed sarcastically. "Hey, don't give me those abandoned-puppy-dog eyes. It's not like we're breakin' up or anything. We just see things differently, and we're each doing our best to get home in our own way. That's all there is to it. Plus, think about it. If all seven of us took a hard-line stance with the grandmaster together, that'd be putting all our eggs in one basket. But if I split off from you guys ahead of time, then we can use that to give us another chance to negotiate down the road if things go south here; you feel me? And Tsukasa knows that, too—it's why he didn't try to stop me."

"I—I mean, you might be right about that, but...even so..."

This wasn't an issue of rationale. It was the act of parting ways itself that filled Akatsuki with fear. There were so many things the Prodigies didn't know about this planet, and having the seven strongest people around all working together had put Akatsuki's heart at ease.

Now he was terrified to lose the arrangement he'd taken for

granted. He tripped over his words, trying desperately to find some way to convince Masato not to go.

"Plus, I don't have anything left I can do for this country."

Masato cut Akatsuki with a quiet remark that was heavy with remorse.

"What do you mean?"

"You heard about the big mess with the currency issuance, right?"

Masato was referring to when Elm tried to mint its new goss currency, and the empire and its other neighbors had cornered the market on raw gold bullion to interfere with Elm's plans.

Thankfully, Masato's ingenuity and Ringo's skills had resolved things without much issue.

"Back then, I was seein' red. If Tsukasa hadn't been so quick on his feet, I woulda ended up destroying the empire's whole economy."

Still, Masato regretted how rashly he had handled things.

"Just now, Tsukasa was talkin' about how politicians gotta look for the better solution, but going after the best *option* is Business 101. Even if you know it'll lead to the worst outcome for someone else, you take that best option, and you run with it. Then you keep on going till your legs give out. That's the way I've lived my life.

"And up till now, that's been fine for us 'cause we've been jump-starting this nation pretty much by brute force. From here on out, though, Elm's gotta learn how to keep the peace with its neighbors and set down roots in the international community. But if a one-man army like me starts butting his head into something like that, all it's gonna do is cause issues for everyone.

"Problem is, I'm not a patient enough guy to sit on my hands and watch other people learn by trial and error. The whole mess with the coinage reminded me of that loud and clear. Even if this thing with Yamato hadn't come up…I'd probably have put some distance between us anyway."

And there was one other thing, too.

"Plus, there's something besides Elm I've got a responsibility toward here."

Akatsuki had a pretty good idea of what Masato was talking about.

"You mean Roo?"

"Yeah. I'm the one who bought her, so it's my job to raise her into a strong enough merchant to be able to buy back her parents. That's something I gotta do myself, and Lakan's got the best seafaring tech this world has to offer. They've got their fingers in pretty much every maritime trading company pie there is, so if there's anywhere I could find where Roo's parents ended up after being taken as slaves from the New World, it's there. That's why I gotta hit the road."

The difference between Tsukasa's methods and Masato's was only one reason why the expert merchant was leaving. The goss trouble had already informed Masato that his disposition and skill set were poorly suited to the task of founding a democratic nation. There was nothing left for him to do here. What's more, he had Roo to think of.

Masato was the only one who shouldered that weight. He was the only one who *could*. Now that the Prodigies had found a way to get home in Neuro, he couldn't afford to put it off. That was why Masato had chosen now to break ranks with the others. After considering what he could provide and all he needed to accomplish, he felt that this was the young man's best option.

"………Man, you guys really are amazing," Akatsuki admitted after listening to Masato's speech.

"How's that?"

"You all know exactly what it is you can do and what needs doing. It feels like…I'm the only one without a clue."

Akatsuki had realized something. It wasn't just Masato; it was everyone. They all knew what the score was. It explained why, when Tsukasa asked Akatsuki if he wanted to keep working together, he hadn't been able to give his answer right away.

Keine had known, as had Aoi. Even Ringo, timid as she was, hadn't hesitated. Shinobu was absent, but Akatsuki was confident she would have been no different if she weren't. So where did that leave the young illusionist?

When Masato announced he was leaving, Akatsuki's mind had gone blank. After Tsukasa hadn't stopped Masato and instead asked the others to consider their positions as well, Akatsuki's legs started trembling. He had thought of their community as unbreakable, and because of that, he had let himself grow dependent on it.

"Unlike you guys, I was just going along with whatever Tsukasa said without thinking twice about it… And now that I have to decide for myself, I'm a mess…"

He had fled in place of giving an actual answer. It was pathetic.

As Akatsuki lambasted himself for his comparative lack of consideration, Masato softly placed a hand on his shoulder.

"Hey, Prince. You mind if I kiss you?"

"WH-WHAAAAAAAAAAAAAAAAT?!?!?!"

Another chill ran up Akatsuki's spine, though this one had a very different feel from the one he'd gotten when Tsukasa asked him how he wished to proceed. He shouted at the top of his lungs.

"Wh-wh-what are you going on about?! Don't be a creep!"

"Nah, you just sounded so much like a chick there that I figured you'd made up your mind to start livin' as a woman."

Akatsuki shook off Masato's hand with all his might.

"Like hell I did! There's something wrong with your brain, man!"

Masato replied with a snarky chuckle—

"…That stuff about you not thinking isn't true, y'know."

—then gave Akatsuki a heartfelt smile and spoke.

"After all, you made a *choice* to believe in Tsukasa. And the only way you could do that was by considerin' things and selecting for yourself that he was someone worth trusting."

"I… I mean, I guess so…"

"So then, what's the problem? If you ask me, there's no quicker way to screw stuff up than to have amateurs tryin' to talk over specialists when they're out of their depth. If it weren't for you keeping your mouth shut and just trusting in Tsukasa, there's no way he woulda been able to unite the people and found a nation so quickly."

Without Akatsuki's help, establishing Elm would have been a much more involved endeavor. Initially, the commoners on the bottom end of this world's power structure thought of "nations" as simply being possessed by the rich and powerful. The notion of collectively leading one hadn't even begun to cross their minds.

Uniting them under a common cause should have been nigh impossible. To them, all of that stuff was just someone else's problem. Yet because Akatsuki was there, the Prodigies had been able to employ the pseudo power structure of religion to unify the populace. That had led directly to the Republic of Elm's birth.

"You can trace all that back to you choosin' to trust Tsukasa. You're not pathetic, Prince. Hell, you might not realize it, but you're actually kinda badass," Masato declared, and it wasn't hollow patronizing, either. All the praise he was heaping on his pip-squeak friend came from the heart. "So…I'm countin' on you to keep looking after Tsukasa for me. He doesn't bend people to his will like I do. He's the kinda guy who can only get stuff accomplished after the people around him buy into it."

That was Masato's parting request—for Akatsuki to keep using his talents to help Tsukasa out.

"…" Akatsuki went silent and looked down for a moment. After a little while, he let out a big breath like he was purging a great weight that had been building up in his chest, looked up, and spoke with his chest held high. "Bwa-ha-ha-ha! Very well! Be off, then, and leave things here to me!"

His voice rang with the dignity of the Seven Luminaries' living deity. All his gloom and helplessness from before had vanished.

"See, that's more like it. Good talk, man." Seeing that his pal was back in high spirits, Masato turned to leave.

As Akatsuki watched his friend go—

"But don't forget!"

—he called out to him one last time.

"When we leave here, we're all doing it together."

Masato glanced back over his shoulder, and Akatsuki stared him straight in the eye. They might have been going their separate ways for now, but this was the one thing Akatsuki refused to back down on.

"...Course."

Masato raised his hand to express his acknowledgment, then set off again. Akatsuki did likewise and began walking back toward the dining room.

The two pairs of footsteps beat at different cadences as they drew farther apart.

As Masato listened to the sound coming from behind him, he whispered, "Sorry, Prince."

The kind smile he had given Akatsuki mere moments ago was gone. All that remained was a gleam in his eyes, as sharp and cold as any knife.

CHAPTER 2

⚜ Ultimate Diplomatic Weapon: Mayo ⚜

Days had passed since Masato left the Seven Luminaries, and spring was in full bloom.

For the Republic of Elm, that meant that the elections were underway.

There were a few conditions to run as a candidate for the National Assembly. You had to be an adult of at least fifteen years of age, be able to read and write, and there was a deposit you had to pay.

The deposit's amount was a trifling sum for any former noble, but it was on par with an entire year's living expenses for a commoner. At first, its announcement earned heavy criticism and accusations of unfairness.

However, nobody was able to rebut Tsukasa's argument that those who lacked the skills to obtain financial backers before the election via the strength of their policy positions and rhetoric would be unable to prevail in the election anyhow. Between that and the desire to limit people from running frivolously, the practice was ultimately implemented.

Once the candidates were decided, they each marched from place to place and spoke of their visions for the nation of Elm in order to garner the masses' support.

Unsurprisingly, the key issue was the Yamato situation, and political aspirants fell primarily into two camps. Some wanted to follow the current provisional government's lead and lend Yamato a hand. Others, however, wanted to leave Yamato to fend for itself to prioritize their relationship with the empire.

In the Findolph domain, where the Seven Luminaries had first started, and the Gustav domain, which owed them a great debt, the popular stance was to honor the Seven Luminaries'—Tsukasa's— example and render aid to Yamato in the name of equality. Meanwhile, the prevailing school of thought in Buchwald and Archride was that the country should acquiesce to the empire's demand and cut ties with Yamato.

Of the two groups, the candidates who urged the importance of helping Yamato became known as Principlists, and those who insisted that their relationship with the empire be prioritized were dubbed Reformists. With the lines so clearly drawn, people on each side of the issue began working together with their like-minded peers, and a pair of political parties were thus formed.

Each was spearheaded by one of the women who had once come to make their case directly to the Seven Luminaries. Tetra led the Principles Party, and Juno ran the Reform Party. They had taken the initiative to share their opinions with the provisional government before anyone else had. In retrospect, it seemed almost inevitable that they were the ones at the center of their respective parties. In the opening stages of the election, neither yielded an inch, and the balance between the two factions was more or less even.

While all that was going on, Tsukasa paid a visit to the Buchwald barracks' dungeon, where prisoners were detained. It was currently home to the pair the election revolved around—First Imperial Yamato Princess Kaguya and White Wolf General Shura.

"Ahhh. ♪ Truly, no food in any land can compare to white rice. ♪"

"*Munch, munch, munch.*"

The cell's stone walls were rough and angular, and it had been hastily furnished with a four-and-a-half-tatami-mat floor. Atop it, Kaguya, Shura, and Tsukasa were sharing a meal.

"When the soldiers told me that you didn't have much of an appetite, I sent to have some rice delivered from Yamato. I see I made the right call."

"Indeed. In this land of the empire—this Republic of Elm now, rather… Whatever its name, the bread they eat in this land in place of rice doth disagree with me. I find it unbearably rough, and it dries the mouth out terribly."

"*Munch, munch, munch.*"

Steam rose from the rice into the cold dungeon air. Shura nodded in agreement with Kaguya as she shoveled the food into her mouth. She was clearly ecstatic, as her white tail wagged restlessly from side to side.

"What a delight it is to know a table filled with Yamato. The pickled *nanohana* hath a wonderful crunch, and their flavor lingers on the tongue just so."

"The miso soup with seaweed is good, too," Shura appended.

"Were it only that we could enjoy it in slightly larger quarters." As she spoke, Kaguya glanced around the cell.

There were tatami mats laid awkwardly across the floor and a low tea table placed atop them to make the Yamato natives feel more at home, but they did little to alleviate the gloom that came from being surrounded by sheer stone on three sides, and the room's sole source of illumination was the scant sunlight that streamed in through the cell bars from above.

It wasn't exactly a view that whetted the appetite. However, the two young women's being held as prisoners in Elm was the only thing keeping them from being deported to the empire, so there was little to be done about it.

"We can't show you too much hospitality, or we risk drawing the empire's ire. I'm afraid you'll have to put up with it," Tsukasa remarked.

"Oh, I know that full well. This white rice is luxury enough for me. Thou hast my thanks, angel." Kaguya gave him an amiable grin.

Tsukasa shrugged. "Think nothing of it. I prefer rice to bread as well, but due to my position, I can't very well ask to have it delivered simply because I want some. That's why I took this opportunity to impose on you like this."

"Is that so?! I suppose it doth only stand to reason that an angel would possess such refined taste. A divine food for a divine tongue! For of all the feasts and delicacies the culinary world hath, none can compare to a bowl of fresh-cooked white rice topped with a single pickled plum. Such is indisputable."

However, as Kaguya sang white rice's praises—

"...Not true."

—Shura spoke up and voiced her dissent.

"Oh?"

"I like barley rice better. Nice and firm. Tasty. Better than white rice."

"Hmph. Thy palate is dull, Shura. The texture of barley rice hath its charm, but doth it not lack the sweetness of white rice that fills thy mouth more with each subsequent bite?"

"How like a weak little princess. Thinking that sweetness is all that matters."

"Why, I never!"

"Barley rice is good for you. Doesn't make you fat. That's why we samurai like it. Also, it goes perfectly with soup. If you pour miso soup over it, the texture gets really nice. But with white rice, it just gets soggy. That's because white rice is weak. Barley rice is stronger and tough. End of discussion."

"Thou aren't even beginning to make sense! If thou art so fond of tough food, then why not just go chew some burdock?!"

"I could say the same to you. If you like sweet things so much, go drink millet jelly."

The two of them stared daggers at each other. Neither was willing to back down.

To look at them, one would hardly guess them to be a princess and her attendant.

If anything, they seem more like a pair of close sisters, Tsukasa mused.

Yet as he watched their good-natured argument play out—

"Angel, settle this! Which do you think is better?!"

"Tell us!"

—he suddenly found himself thrust into the middle of it as each girl looked to gain an advantage by winning him onto their side.

"Good question."

Tsukasa paused for a moment before answering.

"Personally, I prefer rice *cakes* wrapped in seaweed and drizzled with soy sauce."

"Th-that's cheating."

"So it is!"

"By the way, angel, what exactly is the white thing thou hast on thy dish there?"

Midway through their meal, Kaguya pointed at a small tray sitting next to the grilled salmon.

A gleaming, cream-colored goo sat atop its flat surface.

"The other dishes are all from Yamato, but that one alone is new to me. It doth appear far too soft to be tofu."

"…Looks weird."

The two of them timidly prodded at the goo with their chopsticks.

"Ah, you mean the mayonnaise," Tsukasa replied.

""M-mayo…?!""

Kaguya's and Shura's reactions were instantaneous.

The looks on their faces, which mere moments ago had been ones of puzzlement, were replaced with expressions of intense caution.

Hmm?

"Th-the Seven Luminaries' dreaded mayo! 'Tis said that ingesting but a single drop is enough for its effects to take hold, and that it doth possess addictive qualities surpassing those of even the devil's aphrodisiac, opium! A scant few days without it will reduce its victims to invalids, and in the war with the empire, the Seven Luminaries used it to lay countless cities low…!"

"Stay back, Princess. You mustn't eat any. What are you playing at, angel, bringing us something so dangerous?"

"I fear there's been a big misunderstanding."

However, Tsukasa also knew that the blame for that resided close to home. An image of his grinning friend who'd made a pile of messes, then ridden off into the sunset without cleaning any of them up, rose to the forefront of his mind. He was struck by an urge to give it a good, hard kick. Instead, though, he took a piece of salmon, lightly spread some mayonnaise atop it, and took a big bite.

""Aaah!""

"As you can see, as long as it's prepared in a sanitary manner, it doesn't cause addiction or hallucinations or anything of the sort. Mayonnaise is just a condiment made of egg yolk, vinegar, and oil that we Seven Luminaries taught the people about to enrich their lives. I felt that only offering you food you could already get in Yamato wouldn't allow us to show you the full range of our hospitality. I promise, it's quite tasty when spread on the grilled salmon."

After he finished speaking, Tsukasa ate another piece of salmon with mayo.

Seeing that, Kaguya gulped—

"…Very well."

—then took a bit of fish for herself and topped it with mayonnaise while wearing a resolute expression.

"Princess…" Shura gave her an apprehensive gaze.

"As Yamato's rightful empress, 'tis my duty to accept his hospitality with grace," declared Kaguya. "If anything doth happen to me, I leave Yamato's future in thy hands, Shura… *Haumph!*"

Then, after making her dramatic final statement, she shoved the mayo-covered salmon in her mouth.

"OHHH?!"

Her eyes went wide, and she let out a strange cry.

"Princess?!"

"Why, this… What *is* this indescribable flavor?! Sweet? Spicy? Sour, perhaps? In any case…'tis bold! Yet despite that, the harmony it hath with the salmon is impeccable. How delightful! I have never eaten anything like it…!"

"R-really?"

"If thou dost doubt me, Shura, then try some for thyself… Ah, I cannot get enough! Its taste is overpowering in a most agreeable way, and it doth elevate the rice to new heights! First hearing that the Seven Luminaries' god was spreading something white and goopy among his followers made me think ye heretics of the darkest nature, but to learn that this world had such a marvelous food in it!"

Urged on by Kaguya's words, Shura hesitantly ate some mayonnaise.

The moment she did, the shock of experiencing a flavor that shouldn't have even existed in this world touching her taste buds sent a shiver through her entire body. The young *byuma*'s tail puffed up to double its original size.

After that, she was the same as Kaguya.

She began gobbling rice down at twice the rate she had before as though possessed by the mayonnaise's magic.

"Munch, munch! Munch, munch, munch!"

Tsukasa nodded happily when he saw their reactions.

"I'm glad you both like it."

"Indeed! Once Yamato is restored, I insist that you teach me how to— I say, Shura! That one is mine!"

"I'm testing it for poison."

"I've already eaten from it, though! Thou art too late! Return it at once!"

"There might be poison in the bottom half. It's my duty to protect you."

"You dare espouse thy loyalty merely when it serves you?!"

Their chopsticks clashed atop the table as they vied for the last of the mayonnaise.

When Tsukasa watched their undignified battle play out, he was again reminded of mayonnaise's diabolical powers and wondered if, going forward, it might be best to try solving *all* his diplomatic problems with mayonnaise.

He shook his head to rid himself of the dangerous notion.

Eventually, an armistice was reached in the Great Mayonnaise Battle when Tsukasa split the rest of his share between the two combatants.

The three then enjoyed pleasant conversation as they finished their meal, and after the guard cleared away the dishes, they washed down their food with hot tea as they relished the satisfaction of a stomach well filled.

"Ahhh... It hath been some time since I last ate so heartily."

"All full now."

"The mayonnaise was sublime, but the other dishes were fantastic, too. My compliments to the chef."

"For sure."

"You honor me... Hearing you say that makes all the effort I put in worth it."

Kaguya's and Shura's eyes went wide at Tsukasa's response.

"Goodness me. You mean to say that you made our meal yourself?"

"That I do. Cooking is something of a specialty of mine."

"Shocking!"

"I suppose it stands to reason that an angel would be blessed with not just handsome looks and wit enough to run circles around the empire, but culinary skills as well. If you were human, that would make you quite a catch."

"I've heard that there's a custom in Yamato for the master of the house to serve tea to their guests themselves, no matter who holds the higher status," Tsukasa replied. "I'm afraid I don't know much about official tea ceremony rituals, but I think there's a lot to be learned from that ethos."

Kaguya's shoulders shook as she laughed.

"…Heh-heh, what a strange notion. True, we do say that there are no lessers or betters in the tearoom…but that is mere pretense. Unlike the equality for all you preach, it hath no real substance. What exactly is there to learn from that?"

"Pretense is important. It's sad to say, but humans are evil by nature. Without something to hold them back, it's all too easy for them to descend into wickedness. Falsehood, morals, and rules are there to keep them in check. Even if everyone knows they're all smoke and mirrors, they're important nonetheless. It's precisely when charade meets charade that peace can be born."

"Is that not but a false peace brokered between two sides who do not trust each other?" pressed Kaguya.

"Any peace is good peace. True or not, it's still far preferable to war," Tsukasa asserted.

Between lives lost in the name of justice and lives saved through deception, it was clear which outcome was better.

Suddenly, they heard a knock on the door—

"Pardon the intrusion. I've brought the dessert."

—and a maid came down into the dungeon.

When Tsukasa saw her, he stood up and opened the cell to let her in. She set the table, and he thanked her and quietly dismissed the woman. Then he returned to his seat and gestured at the plates. Each one was covered with small yellow discs.

"These are some potato cakes I made with sweet potatoes from Yamato."

They were a kind of tea cake enjoyed all across Yamato. Rich and poor alike adored them.

When Kaguya and Shura saw desserts—

"Potato cakes..."

"..."

—they merely stared at them for some reason. Neither moved to take a bite.

"...Would you have preferred something else?" Tsukasa inquired.

Kaguya shook her head. "Oh, no, nothing of the sort. They simply brought back memories."

"Of what, exactly?"

"I once knew a man skilled at serving tea. His brew itself was good, but his potato cakes were truly something else... Someday, I hope the time comes when I may eat them again."

"No more talking about him," Shura interjected sharply. "He was a samurai general, but he sided with your sister and betrayed you and the Yamato people anyway. I'll never forgive him for what he did. He's a stain on my family, and I swear I'll cut him down myself."

Shura's eyes were cast downward, and she spoke in a voice so low it was like she was cursing the very air itself.

Kaguya shrugged awkwardly. "My apologies. 'Tis hardly an appropriate topic for this table you've so graciously prepared. I hope you can forgive us."

"Think nothing of it. Things don't always turn out well, even when it comes to family." After waving off Kaguya's apology, Tsukasa forcibly changed the subject. "However, I will agree that it doesn't particularly pique my interest. I don't know what happened between you, your parents, and your siblings, or why you stand on opposite sides now, but that's all in the past. I came here today to talk about the future."

He looked Kaguya right in the eyes, and she responded by straightening her posture.

"I see. So this is the true reason behind your visit?"

Tsukasa nodded. "As a member of the Seven Luminaries and as the head of Elm's current provisional government…I'm here to give my answer regarding your request that we free Yamato."

"My, my, such pageantry. If ye would hold to the righteousness your god upholds, is not your answer a foregone conclusion?" Once again, Kaguya was using the Seven Luminaries' fundamental principle of equality for all as a negotiating tool.

Without its tenets, an organization had no reason to keep existing. That was as true of Elm as it was of anything. Kaguya's threat was an indirect one, but it was a threat all the same. Yet Tsukasa wasn't the least bit shaken by it.

"Let me cut to the chase: Elm will not be fighting the empire on Yamato's behalf."

"…Oh?" Kaguya narrowed her gaze.

"At the moment, Elm and Freyjagard have a peace treaty and are hard at work fostering friendly relations with each other. Destroying all that would carry tremendous costs for Elm."

"Ye angels would abandon my nation to ruin, then?"

"Eras come and go, and every dynasty eventually falls. The way I see it, Yamato's time has come. You have my sympathies."

However, it was a ruler's final duty to go down with the ship.

Just like in any organization, a leader was a person whose job it was to take responsibility.

Whenever something went wrong, they were the ones who had to shoulder the blame.

That was true even if they bore no fault of their own.

Their taking on that cost was the reason they were afforded such privilege in the first place.

As such, Kaguya's current situation was a natural conclusion of that.

However…

"However, your people are another matter."

"Hmm?"

"When an autocracy falls, it isn't the fault of its citizens. Guilt can't be leveled upon those who lacked the ability to prevent something from occurring.

"As such, if the people of old Yamato genuinely are suffering under the dominion government's rule, then Elm will freely offer them its aid.

"We've gotten in contact with the dominion government, and we've requested to visit them in person.

"They'll want to take the opportunity to try to convince me to turn you over, so I have no reason to believe they'll refuse.

"Once we're there, I'll use the opportunity to see for myself what state the dominion is in. If what you say is true, and they really do need help, we intend to demand that the dominion and imperial governments amend the situation at once, and if necessary, we're prepared to offer technological aid and financial relief to help make that happen.

"In the name of equality for all, we'll ensure that the people of old Yamato can expect a reasonable quality of life and to have their fundamental human rights respected. That is what we're prepared to offer your people. No more and no less."

"In short, you mean to say that ye Seven Luminaries are allies to the 'people' but will do nothing for Yamato as a 'nation'?"

Tsukasa nodded. "That's exactly right. The Seven Luminaries are in the business of saving *people*, not countries. Reestablishing a fallen nation would carry a level of risk that we're unwilling to assume. We simply have no reason to go to such lengths for Yamato. And in keeping with that… To put it bluntly, if the empire demands that they be allowed to interrogate you in exchange for bettering the conditions of the Yamato populace, we're prepared to consider hand-ing you over."

"_____"

The moment the words left Tsukasa's mouth, bloodlust flared up in Shura's gaze beneath her dangling forelocks.

However—

"'Tis fine."

—Kaguya verbally held the White Wolf General in check, then replied to Tsukasa.

"If my life is enough to ensure the safety of my citizens, then as Yamato's rightful ruler, I can imagine no greater joy than to lay it down for them. If ye angels tell me with surety that my sacrifice will safeguard my people, then I shall have no reason to refuse."

Kaguya's words made it clear that she, too, was acting for the sake of her subjects rather than trying to reclaim the Yamato imperial fam-ily's lost glory. It was an exemplary response.

When you were relying on the other party's goodwill, you needed to convey to them that your intentions were honorable as well. Whether Kaguya was lying didn't matter, for it was the only reply she could have given. Still, Tsukasa was impressed by how she had stated so without a hint of trepidation in her eyes. He could tell that she pos-sessed the valuable combination of wisdom and courage.

"...But I must say, I feel a trifle let down," Kaguya admitted, con-tinuing with a disappointed smile. "All this pedestrian talk of risk and return. When I came to ye Seven Luminaries, I had assumed that ye would merely use your divine powers unconstrained by the limits of man to see justice meted out in an instant. But this, why, it feels as though I'm talking to a mere mortal."

"Well, that makes sense. We *are* only human, after all," Tsukasa said plainly.

"…What?"

Tsukasa had to agree that this was anything but what an outsider like Kaguya might have anticipated.

Kaguya's and Shura's expressions froze as though they had just been punched in the backs of their heads.

After lowering his voice, Tsukasa elaborated. "I've already cleared the area…and I trust that what I'm about to tell you can stay between us."

Tsukasa told the pair how he and the other Prodigies came from Earth, a planet where technology was far more advanced. He revealed their search for a way to get back home and how battling the empire became necessary in the process. Then he explained how Grandmaster Neuro ul Levias was from another world as well—and that he possessed a way to send them back to Earth. Tsukasa recounted everything that had happened to him and the other Prodigies since the plane crash.

"A village saved our lives when we first arrived, and all the fighting we've done since then has been to repay that kindness. The only reason we called ourselves gods and angels was because it made our words more convincing. Doing so was necessary to build a nation where our saviors could live their lives in peace."

""………""

Tsukasa spared no detail, even going so far as to expose the fact that the Prodigies had deceived the world. The dungeon cell was silent save for his confession of the truth behind the fake Seven Luminaries. Kaguya and Shura didn't say a word. They just listened.

"Have I dashed your hopes?" Tsukasa asked once he had finished.

With a cautious gaze, Kaguya responded, "…Why wouldst thou tell us this?"

She didn't understand. If what Tsukasa was telling her was true, then it was a massive weakness for both the Seven Luminaries and for the Republic of Elm as a whole. If these facts came to light, the Seven Luminaries would lose credibility; it could even lead to Elm's collapse.

Tsukasa should have been guarding this secret with his life. And yet here he was, baring it freely. Kaguya couldn't figure out what his motive was, and that put her on guard.

Perhaps sensing as much, Tsukasa tried to elaborate. "If I didn't lead with that, it would make it difficult for me to address the main reason I'm here."

"There's more…?"

"As I just told you, we built the Republic of Elm for our saviors—no, our friends—from this world. However, once the elections we're holding decide the National Assembly, and we hand over power from the provisional government to the citizens, the vast bulk of our work will be done, and we'll no longer have any reason to remain here. And with Grandmaster Neuro ul Levias already having offered us a way to get back to our original world, the only thing we'll have left to do at that point is to take him up on his offer… *However*." Tsukasa took a sip of his green tea to wet his lips, then continued. "At the same time, I can't help but feel that we have left something unresolved."

"What dost you mean…?"

"The thing is: We don't even know the reason we were brought to this planet in the first place. Departing before solving that mystery will leave us with regret. I have an uneasy feeling in my gut about that, and I've learned to trust my gut. I need to know—who sent us here and why?"

Tsukasa and the other Prodigies had been tracking down leads on a pair of phrases that seemed related to those questions. He asked Kaguya about them point-blank.

"Do you know anything about either the Seven Heroes or an evil dragon?"

This was what Tsukasa had truly hoped to discuss. Those phrases were the only clues he and his friends had about who had summoned them to this world.

"...The Seven Heroes or an evil dragon?" After Kaguya repeated the words back, she tilted her head. "I have not heard of them. Shura, what about thou?"

Shake, shake.

Shura was in the same boat. She shook her head no. She didn't know anything, either.

"...I see."

Tsukasa let out a sigh, dejection welling up within him.

Several centuries ago, the emperor of Freyjagard decided that no higher entity than he could be allowed to exist and conducted a religious purge. All the information on the original Seven Luminaries, which likely held ties to the Seven Heroes and the evil dragon, went up in smoke. Shinobu was in the empire trying to see if she could find anything out about them, but the fact that she hadn't called with good news yet spoke to just how thorough the purge had been.

However, Kaguya's nation of Yamato had a long history and sat on the same continent as the empire. Tsukasa had been hoping that some of the erased Seven Luminaries knowledge or teachings had secretly survived there. Regrettably, that didn't seem to be the case, and he was right back to square—

"...Ah! No, no! Hold on a moment!"

Then, it happened. Out of the blue, Kaguya raised her voice, rested her finger against her shapely jawline, sank into thought—

"...Ah, the evil dragon. I have heard a phrase bearing a similar nuance before."

—and then finally answered.

"You have?!" Tsukasa exclaimed.

"When I was but a babe, and my mother was yet alive, she told me that Yggdra doth not like bad children—and that a mean old dragon would gobble them up."

"Is that from some Yamato fairy tale? A legend told to children to get them to behave?" Tsukasa pressed.

Shura shook her head. "I don't think so. I've never heard of it."

"My mother was of a minor tribe of elves skilled in magic who lived in the forest. See how my ears are different from those of normal *hyuma*?" Kaguya tapped on her long, pointed ear with her fingertip.

"This is apparently a feature of the tribe, and those rich in elven blood can use their large ears to hear the voices of spirits. My mother's kin kept to themselves for the most part. As I recall, her generation was the first to so much as interact with the Yamato government. 'Tis hardly a surprise they would have their own oral tradition and beliefs. I imagine the phrase about Yggdra is part of that."

"_____"

Kaguya's revelation stunned Tsukasa into silence. It was all connected. No, he couldn't jump to conclusions. There wasn't enough information to say that for sure yet. Tsukasa could feel it, though. For the first time since waking up stranded here, he was close. The truth about the long-lost Seven Luminaries Winona had told him about was nearer than ever before.

And of particular note was that bit about the elves.

After all, the feature Kaguya just mentioned…was something that could be said of Lyrule, too. The mysterious person who had called the Prodigies the Seven Heroes had spoken through her back at Castle Findolph.

Tsukasa was pretty sure it was no coincidence that they had crash-landed near Lyrule, and now he'd discovered that a group of people with heritage similar to hers lived in the forests of Yamato. Even more conspicuous was how a phrase from their oral tradition mentioned an entity resembling the evil dragon.

This is something I need to look into.

Tsukasa rose from his seat and looked out the lattice window toward the blue sky.

"Perhaps the land of Yamato might hold some of the answers we're looking for, after all."

Their meal and discussion were finished, and Tsukasa had left the dungeon cell. Now that the two young women from Yamato were alone, Shura posed a question to her master.

"…Are you sure about this, Princess?"

"Sure about what?"

"We could have tried to trade that information for his help."

"I quite doubt it." Kaguya's reply was immediate. Trying that wouldn't have gotten them anywhere. "If he were the sort of man to steer his nation merely to serve his ends, he would have turned us over to the empire long ago. From what he said, their relationship with Neuro is akin to a lifeline. Despite that, he agreed to help Yamato's people all the same, albeit not with blade in hand. Even with the risk of angering Neuro looming, he chose to act for the sake of his country's future."

Kaguya could tell that Tsukasa was the sort of man ready to take extreme measures to avoid behaving selfishly. He claimed to be mortal...but that mentality of his could very well be described as angelic. It didn't seem human, that was for sure. To put it bluntly, the integrity he conducted himself with was downright unsettling.

"A man like that would never accept such a deal."

"What about threatening to tell people he isn't an angel, then?" Shura inquired.

"That would prove equally fruitless. True or not, 'tis the people who ultimately choose to believe. Our accusing the Seven Luminaries of deceit will hardly cause the populace's faith in them to waver. Were that not so, that man would never have revealed the truth to us."

Kaguya and Shura could say whatever they pleased, but getting folks to believe them was another task entirely. Tsukasa hadn't left the pair a single chip to bargain with. From a diplomatic standpoint, Kaguya's side had suffered a crushing defeat.

And yet...

"'Tis of no concern, though. We have no need for such wheeling and dealing in the first place." As she spoke, Kaguya's gorgeous lips curled into a faint smile.

"Huh?"

"Our conversation made that quite evident. That man hath aims not just to found a nation, but to *change this world's very way of being.* Thou shalt not commit acts of violence. Thou shalt not steal. Thou shalt not violate others.

"He intends to take the morals that *only exist between those of even standing* and use his philosophy of equality to elevate them to

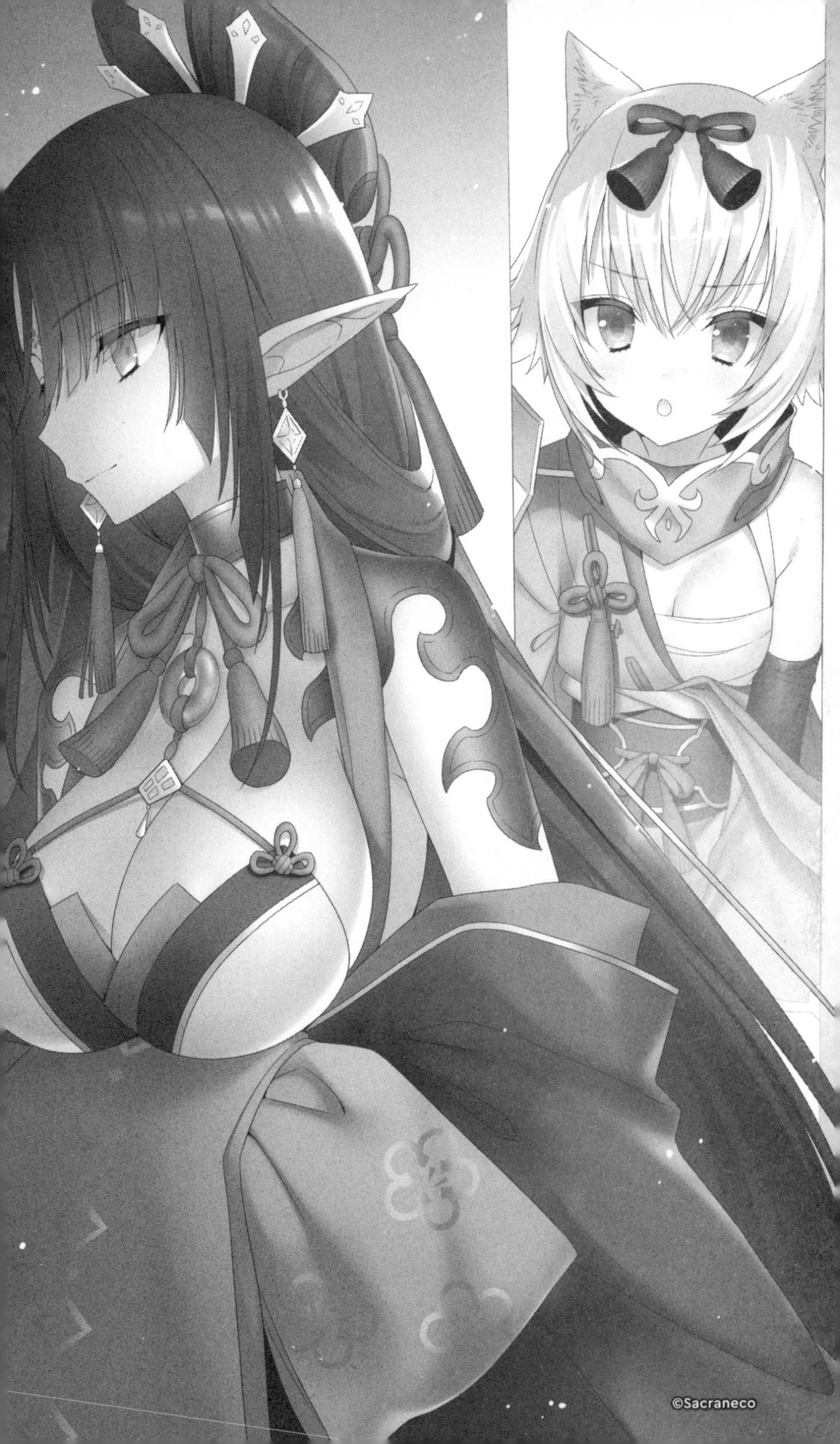

ubiquitous ideals. To create a land where they are seen as inviolable principles, accepted and taken for granted by all.

"To usher in an era of peace, built atop a mountain of deceit."

People wouldn't trust one another.

They wouldn't accept those who were different.

However, because they didn't want to be mocked and decried as immoral barbarians, they would begrudgingly compromise anyway.

Tsukasa had said that even that kind of peace was far preferable to demanding justice violently. However, that was precisely why Kaguya knew that it wouldn't work out. Once Tsukasa learned what Yamato was like now, he would have no choice but to accept as much, too.

He wanted to make a world where humanitarianism was a universally accepted constant. But if that was his goal...then war with Mayoi, current lord of the Yamato dominion, was inevitable.

"Hatred foolish enough to level nations cannot be permitted to exist in his new world," Kaguya muttered with such grief it almost sounded like she would begin to sob.

That evening, Tsukasa called Prodigy journalist Shinobu Sarutobi, who had infiltrated the Freyjagard Empire under the guise of being an exchange student, on his satellite phone.

"Hey, hey, hey! It's your girl Shinobu, reporting live from Drachen. What's up?"

"Shinobu, do you have a moment?"

"Yup! Just takin' a bath right now."

"...Should I call back later, then?"

"Nah, it's all good. I got Ringo to make my phone waterproof, and

I've got it on speaker, so my hands are free, too. FYI, I'm lathering up my boobs right now."

"Why the play-by-play, exactly?"

"Figured I should start throwing in some fanservice every now and then."

"That…won't be necessary." Tsukasa frowned, then got down to brass tacks. The purpose of his call was to compare notes with Shinobu. He started by telling her everything that had happened over the last few days. Between Kaguya's intrusion, Masato's departure, and the things he'd learned from Kaguya, there was a lot to unpack.

"…Ah." After listening in silence, Shinobu let out a sigh. *"So Massy's already left for Lakan with Roo?"*

"He has. I knew that the work I had him doing wasn't exactly his speed, but…I didn't realize he took the goss incident so hard."

"He might not look it, but Massy regards his work seriously. The way he sees it, cutting people from assignments they're not a good fit for is a basic part of project management. Course, Roo's situation probably played into his choice to head for Lakan, too."

Tsukasa paused for a moment before replying to Shinobu's assessment. "…Yes, I imagine so."

"?"

Shinobu had expected him to answer immediately, and Tsukasa could feel her suspicion through the smartphone, but—

"Lakan has a de facto monopoly on this world's shipping industry. If he wants to know what came from the New World and where it went, heading to Lakan is the quickest way to do that."

—instead of explaining his pause, he simply elaborated on the reason for his agreement.

"Anyhoo, I think that gets me up to speed on Massy. And it's him we're talking about, so I'm sure he'll be fine on his own," Shinobu responded, choosing not to press the issue. She trusted Tsukasa. If

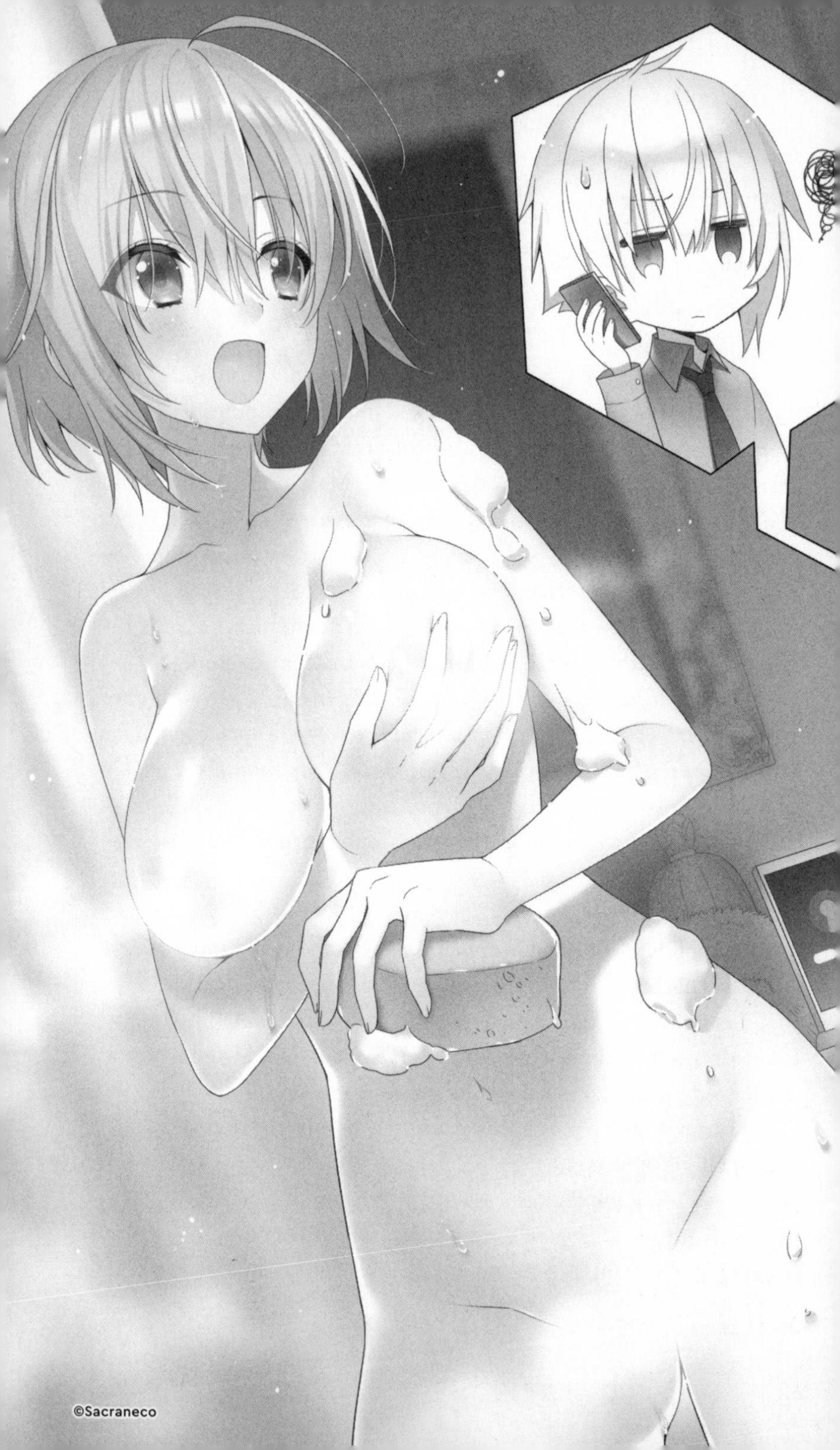

there was something he wasn't saying, it was because he'd decided that it didn't need to be revealed. Instead, Shinobu shifted the conversation to a more pressing matter.

"...Plus, I think Princess Kaguya's story deserves some thought."

This time, Tsukasa's answer came promptly.

"Not only does a species called elves with features similar to Lyrule's live in Yamato, but that race has a phrase used to admonish children that bears a striking similarity to the legends we know about the Seven Luminaries... Given Yamato and Freyjagard's geographic relationship, I suppose it only makes sense that people fled there to avoid the religious purge."

"So there's a pretty good chance that this tribe's beliefs might be the OG Seven Luminaries'?"

"I don't have any firm evidence, but I think it's a real possibility."

"Sorry, I know this would all be easier if I could just find a smoking gun for you. Like, if I discovered that this Yggdra who Kaguya mentioned was the entity the Seven Luminaries worshiped or something. But so far, I haven't been able to find a single thing past what Winona already told us—that the Seven Heroes came from another world, beat the evil dragon, and saved the day. People 'round here are still in panic mode over Kaguya asking Elm for help, so I haven't had the chance to really dig into the Seven Luminaries or the Seven Heroes. Sorry 'bout that."

Shinobu's tone was apologetic, but Tsukasa told her not to worry about it. Tensions between Elm and Freyjagard were high because of Kaguya, so Tsukasa had requested that Shinobu prioritize ensuring their exchange students were safe over everything else. It was hardly her fault that she didn't have much time to dedicate to gathering intel. Still, they didn't call her a Prodigy journalist for nothing. Despite the adverse conditions, Shinobu hadn't come up completely empty-handed.

"I do have a tidbit, though... After doing a little digging on Grand-master Neuro, I turned up something that caught my attention."

"Go on..."

"Honestly, I'd be surprised if you weren't wondering this already, too. Why do you suppose Freyjagard would even want to invade Yamato?"

"That question has been on my mind lately. From what I've gathered, Yamato was a nation that valued honorable poverty," answered Tsukasa. "It didn't have any major industries or natural resources, but it *was* known for its unique samurai and ninja military forces. If it were a fish, it would be one with little meat and lots of jagged bones that made for poor eating whether simmered or fried. Freyjagard going out of its way to gobble it up seemed peculiar, to say the least. And it's apparent that they're still having trouble governing the region to this day."

At first, the empire fully annexed Yamato into itself, but between the region's low economic merits and the active danger posed by its resistance movement, nearly all imperial nobles refused to take the domain as their own. Ultimately, it was left as a self-governing dominion. Observing the facts certainly made it seem as though the empire's invasion had been for nothing.

"Are you saying that Neuro was involved somehow?"

"Apparently, it was the Four Grandmasters who pushed for the invasion in the first place."

"...Is that so?"

"Yeah, and even at the time, the aristocracy wasn't too happy about it. I barely even had to look to find out that most of the noble big shots brought complaints about the campaign to Emperor Lindworm himself. All the stuff you just brought up—they did, too. But Neuro and the other grandmasters pushed Lindworm to start the war, and because they'd been loyal to him since day one, he chose to listen to them."

According to Shinobu, the grandmasters had insisted on the matter, and the friction that caused between the blue bloods and them was a big factor in their current power struggle.

"Don't you think that's weird?"

"Yeah. Something smells fishy."

No matter how you sliced it, something was off about the whole situation.

"It doesn't take a political mastermind to know that invading a country with few resources but a robust military is a wasteful decision. And Neuro claimed that his primary goal was to be able to live in peace. It should have given him even less of a motive to attack Yamato."

"Yet he and the other grandmasters were the ones who were pushing for the assault. And that means…"

"…There was something in Yamato they needed above all else, even if it meant creating a fierce enemy in their own backyard."

Neuro's goal hadn't been to take Yamato for himself. If that was the case, he'd be ruling it already. Thus, it wasn't land he sought, but something else.

"No clue what he's after, though. But ever since the emperor left Neuro in charge, all the policies he's enacted have been moderate and sensible. He doesn't favor the commoners, the nobles—nobody. And that makes it tough to get a sense of what kinda guy he is. Yet for how hard to pin down he is everywhere else…it looks like he really pressed for the Yamato invasion. If we start researching why, I think it'll paint a pretty clear picture of who exactly Neuro ul Levias is."

"That's your intuition as a ninja talking?"

"As a journalist, more like!"

"I see. Well, I know better than to doubt *that*. The work you did for me in Japan taught me that much." Tsukasa smiled faintly as he recalled how Shinobu had helped him expose political corruption—and not just in enemy factions, but within his own party as well.

Her ability to sniff out wrongdoing in places he didn't think to look was invaluable. Coming to another world hadn't changed that.

"You're right—uncovering that reason is important, as is knowing more about Neuro. For now, I want you to concentrate your efforts on his background. Digging up intel on the Seven Luminaries and the Legend of the Seven Heroes will be easier for you once we unearth more on our end."

"How're you gonna do that?" Shinobu asked, puzzled.

"The dominion government got in touch with Elm through Freyjagard to inform us that they want to discuss turning over Kaguya and Shura. I'm heading down to Yamato myself tomorrow for that meeting, and while I'm there, I also plan on looking into the aforementioned minor tribe."

"…You sure that's a good idea? You aren't afraid they'll attack you if you refuse to hand 'em over?"

"Yamato's former second imperial princess, Mayoi, might have been put in charge of ruling, but it's still a dominion of the empire. Freyjagard is trying to cultivate a strong relationship with Elm, and there's no reason for Yamato to go against the empire's orders. Aggression wouldn't benefit them. I can't imagine them stepping that far out of line."

After reassuring her, though—

"…If anything, I'm more concerned about what the Republic of Elm will do."

—Tsukasa went on in a voice tinged with sorrow.

"Huh? How's that?"

"Elm has talked a big game about democracy, but up until now, it's been a democracy in name alone. We've ruled as despots, using the shadow of our overwhelming strength to drag the country along whether it wanted to come or not. All of that changes now, however. Starting with the national elections, Elm will begin walking on its own two feet and choosing its path for the first time. And when it does…things are going to come to a head. Between democracy and the malice that follows in its wake."

Tsukasa's voice was firm. This was something he was confident of. He knew precisely what was about to happen to the fledgling nation. And he understood that there was no way to avoid it, no matter how hard the Prodigies tried, for there was an intractable evil that dwelled within the nature of humanity.

"This is going to be do-or-die for the Republic of Elm."

CHAPTER 3

❧ The Yamato Dominion ❧

It was just past the peak of spring, when the blue of the sky was growing brighter by the day. The Republic of Elm received a message from the Yamato dominion stating that they wished to discuss the future of Elm's prisoner Kaguya—one of the last survivors of the Yamato imperial family and the leader of the resistance movement trying to liberate Yamato.

Its contents were as follows:

Kaguya's accusations are baseless, and there is no truth whatsoever to her claim that the empire oppresses the people of Yamato. The Yamato dominion government's rule is just and fair, and we would like to demonstrate that fact to you. Instead of listening to Kaguya's slander, we ask that Elm come to see how Yamato is doing with its own eyes.

In short, they were calling Kaguya a liar and inviting representatives from Elm to verify as much in person. The Elm provisional government had no reason to turn them down, so the Prodigies agreed immediately. Thus, Tsukasa and a group of other officials from the provisional administration got in Ringo Oohoshi's off-road truck and headed down to the Yamato dominion.

"Ahhh… The breeze feels nice, that it does," Aoi remarked in an elated tone with her head out a window, hair waving in the wind. "It poured for nearly a week, but the rain clouds parted on the very day of our departure. Surely this is a good omen, Tsukasa, m'lord."

Tsukasa, who was sitting beside her and driving, nodded. "It really is. Even by truck, the trip to Yamato will take a while. The lack of asphalt in this world makes driving unpleasant under the best of conditions, but it would have been even worse if it were still raining. Of course, the precipitation has left the path in a sorry state, but— Ack!"

The truck's frame shook, interrupting him. Because the ground was covered in puddles, it was difficult to see where the bumps in the terrain were. Tsukasa grimaced, having almost bitten his tongue, but Aoi didn't seem particularly fazed.

"Ha-ha-ha. I am well acquainted with poor roads. These remind me of the ones Lady Keine and I traveled on back in the Middle East. That land was full of rocks and cliffs as far as the eye could see; that it was."

"And sand, I imagine."

"Indeed, and the heat waves were nigh unbearable. Our vehicles would get as hot as frying pans, and merely touching them would be enough to scald the skin. Compared to that, I daresay this is almost comfortable. The ride is pleasantly bumpy, and the wind is nice and warm… Why, it's making me…a bit…drowsy…that it is…"

"I'm not enough of a stickler to say that it's rude to doze off while riding shotgun, but if you're going to take a nap, you should at least close the window first. Warm or not, you're liable to catch a cold like that."

"Zzz…"

"…Out like a light, huh?"

Tsukasa was impressed at how relaxed Aoi looked. Being able

to sleep that soundly in a truck that bounced up and down every few seconds was no small feat. Such was to be expected of a Prodigy swordmaster who had fought on battlefields the world over.

However...Aoi Ichijou wasn't some big, brawny man. She was a young woman—and one who could easily be described as beautiful. Tsukasa gave her a sidelong glance. In his opinion, she could have stood to pay a little more attention to the way other people saw her.

Even now, the vehicle's shaking was causing her kimono to come loose, leaving her shoulders bare. Each time the truck jolted, the situation worsened. Before long, her robe seemed liable to fall all the way down to her breasts.

Aoi herself might not have minded, but it left Tsukasa with a lack of places to rest his gaze as the person sitting next to her.

"Ringo, would you mind reaching forward and putting a blanket on her? I don't know how much good sleeping in here is going to do, but if anything happens in Yamato, her combat prowess will be our lifeline. Any rest she gets now may pay dividends later."

"You...got it."

Ringo pulled out a comforter from beneath her seat and draped it over Aoi in her unladylike state. Despite the constant jostling, Aoi continued peacefully snoozing away.

As Tsukasa watched out of the corner of his eye, he thought of a question. "By the way, Ringo, I know I asked you to come so I could get an engineer's perspective on the state of Yamato's soil and water quality, as well as its infrastructure, but are you sure you have everything necessary to do that? If there's other tools or anything you need, make sure you speak up before we cross the border."

Three years ago, Yamato was the site of a ferocious war, and much of its infrastructure had been damaged or destroyed. Checking to make sure it had been adequately mended and was back in good

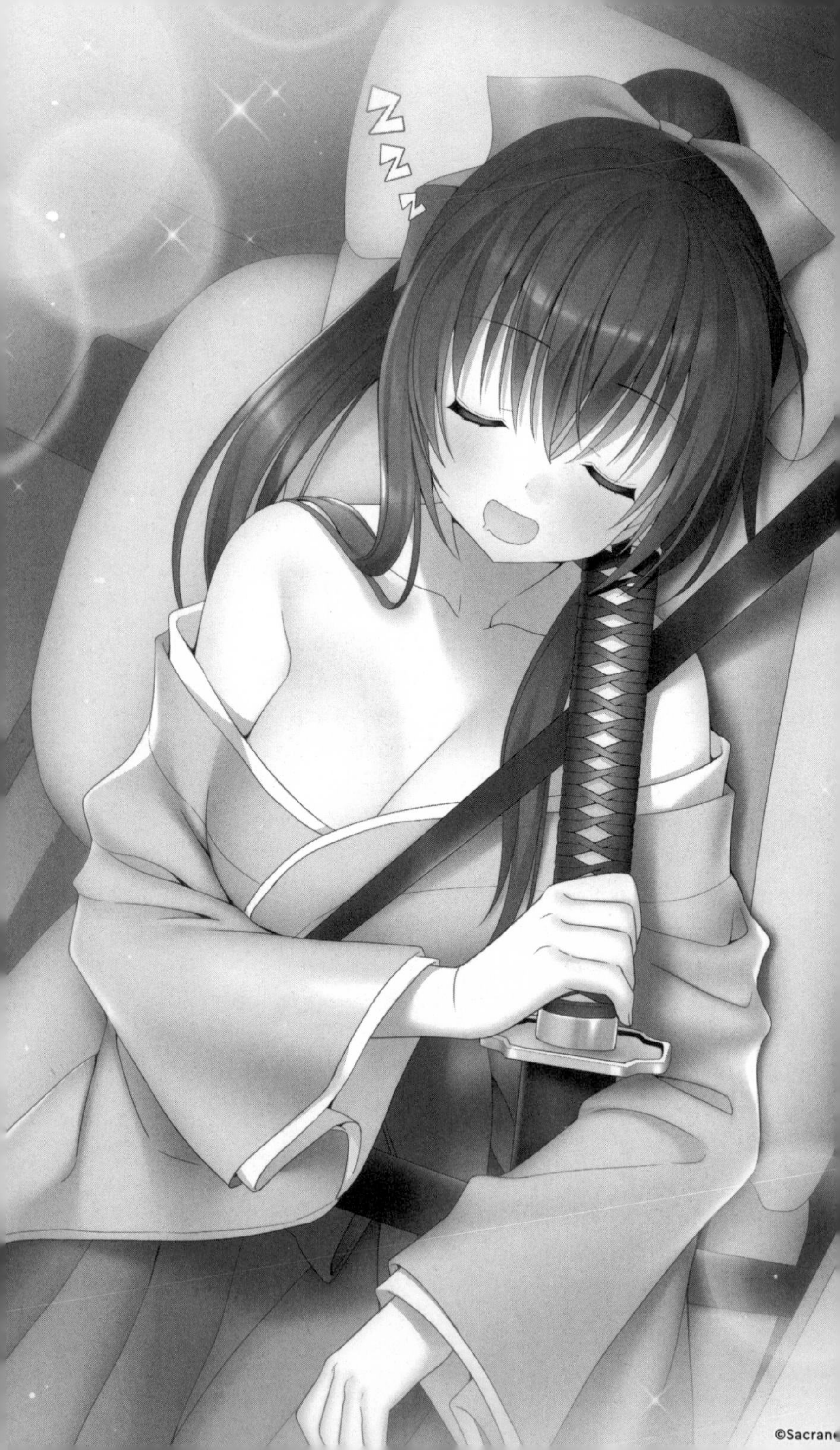
ZZZ
©Sacran

working order was an essential goal of their trip. However, Tsukasa and the others had left on fairly short notice.

It wouldn't be odd for Ringo to be under-equipped. Tsukasa had inquired just to make sure, but Ringo shook her head no.

"I'm...all good. I gathered up...everything I thought I'd need... before we left."

"I see you're on top of things as always. I shouldn't have even asked... Not long ago, there was a large-scale armed conflict in Yamato. If the empire left the destroyed infrastructure as is—and is letting it negatively impact the Yamato people's quality of life— we need to know. I want you to be as thorough as possible in your inspections."

"B-but...even if I have the tools... Will they really...let us do that research?"

According to Kaguya, the empire was oppressing the people of Yamato. If that was true, then the easiest way to prove it would be by examining how healthy the populace was and observing their living conditions. However, the Yamato government was unlikely to cooperate. They might try to sweep all the uncomfortable truths under the rug and only show the Prodigies places that fit their narrative. In Ringo's mind, that seemed alarmingly likely.

However...

"I've certainly considered that prospect, but I don't think we need to worry too much about that sort of ad hoc trickery," Tsukasa stated.

"Why...not?"

"As much as politicians might think themselves invincible, it's always harder to control the citizenry than they think."

No matter how fiercely you ordered someone to smile, it was impossible to erase fear's dark shadow from their face. Tsukasa had seen no shortage of those hollow, fake grins in his time as Japan's prime minister. That was what made him so confident. The possibility that he might fail to spot a facade masking fright and revulsion hadn't even crossed his mind.

"I won't let them get away with any sort of flimsy deception. After all, they're the ones who invited us to see things for ourselves. If they're going to let me conduct an inspection, then that's precisely what they will get. Don't worry, though. I plan on handling all the negotiations myself, so don't feel guilty about entrusting that part to me."

"U-um, if I may…"

While Tsukasa and Ringo spoke, the girl sitting beside the genius inventor raised her hand timidly. Her blond hair and blue eyes set off her attractive complexion, but her most notable feature was her long, pointed ears. Indeed—it was the Prodigies' friend and savior, Lyrule. Those beautiful eyes of hers wavered with uncertainty as she addressed Tsukasa.

"I understand why you asked Aoi and Ringo to come, but why me?"

"As I told you, I want you here as an ambassador of the Republic of Elm," Tsukasa replied.

"B-but I'm just a simple country girl. I can't be someone as important as an a-ambassador…"

"That's not true at all. You're one of the core members who's been helping Elm fight for its independence since day one. You're more than qualified to represent its provisional government. Furthermore, Elm is holding its inaugural elections, which means that the provisional government's standing is questionable. Suppose the delegation we send to this negotiation is compromised solely of us inhuman 'angels.' In that case, Yamato's government might turn around later and break any agreements we make, citing that, without any mortals, the concerned parties didn't have proper representation."

Having accords broken through questionable sophistry was par for the course when it came to international diplomacy. It was best to avoid giving the other side anything to work with.

"B-but…" Lyrule still wasn't totally sold on Tsukasa's explanation. "…If that's the case, then surely Winona or Mayor Ulgar would be better…and more of an adult."

"Absolutely not," Tsukasa shot back.

"Why not?"

"To put it bluntly, they're completely uncultured."

"Th-that really was blunt!"

Tsukasa went on, not mincing his words in the slightest. "They can't read and don't know how to speak formally, and they have no interest in learning how. You certainly could try to teach them, but the moment you blinked, they'd run off chasing wild boars. There's no way we could let someone like that be the public face of our nation. We'd look like idiots."

A long, heavy sigh escaped Tsukasa's lips. Since the very beginning, the villagers had been with the Prodigies, and Tsukasa had made efforts to cultivate them into more refined people. However, each of his attempts had concluded in bitter failure.

"Out of all the Elm villagers, the only ones qualified to be our ambassador are you and Elch, but Elch has his work with the Ministry of Finance to take care of, so I can't put any more on his plate. And although Heiseraat and Archride joined the revolution partway through, they have the same issue as Elch. You're the only person I can count on. Besides, we'll be taking care of the inspections and negotiations. You can just sit back and enjoy your status as a representative."

"Y-you make it sound so easy, but…" Despite the young man's reassurances, Lyrule was still worried about a country girl like her being entrusted with such a meaningful title.

Hoping to placate her, Tsukasa offered another explanation.

"I promise, you really don't need to think that hard about it.

Honestly, the true reason I asked you to come along had less to do with filling the ambassador title and more to do with me wanting your help with something else."

"Huh?"

There was something more important than being Elm's ambassador? Lyrule looked at Tsukasa with a mix of surprise and confusion.

"Do you remember what happened to you back when Gustav attacked Dormundt with his war magic?"

"O-of course I do," Lyrule answered with a big nod.

A strange woman's voice had come out of nowhere and asked her to protect Tsukasa and the other Seven Heroes from Gustav's war magic. Then, immediately afterward, she became able to use magic and hear the voices of spirits. The strange occurrence was still shrouded in mystery. However, there was no questioning the fact that it had changed Lyrule's life in a big way. Forgetting it was impossible.

"...And while I don't remember it myself, there was another strange event just like it in Castle Findolph, right? While I was passed out, I mean," said Lyrule.

"Exactly." Tsukasa nodded before continuing. "Based on the information and legends we found while looking for a way to return home, I've concluded that there's a set of three rules that this world operates under.

"Rule 1: There existed some sort of threat to the world referred to as the evil dragon.

"Rule 2: There existed some sort of entity that opposed the evil dragon.

"Rule 3: There existed a group known as the Seven Heroes affiliated with the opposer that was called in from somewhere beyond.

"Of those, we're the group from Rule 3, and our working theory is that the mysterious voice who keeps using you as a medium to contact us—that is to say, the being from Rule 2—might well be the entity that summoned us to this planet in the first place. Then, this Rule 2 being borrowed your voice and called us the Seven Heroes. Shinobu's investigations have revealed that they're the basis of the original Seven Luminaries' religion that was once practiced across this continent. In other words, there's an incredibly high chance that this entity from Rule 2 is related to the Seven Luminaries in some capacity."

If it turned out that this minor tribe of elves was indeed a group of Seven Luminaries worshippers who had avoided the purge, then it stood to reason that the land of Yamato held a close connection to the being from Rule 2. As such...

"By entering Yamato, we might have a chance to make definitive contact with them. And given that all the previous times we've interacted have been through you, I suspect that there's some quality you possess that makes you essential for contacting the entity."

"Really...?"

"Yes. I requested that you join us as an ambassador so that we'll know right away if the being contacts you. I don't know why all our previous interactions with them have been so choppy and fragmented, but if we could hold a solid conversation, I suspect it could clear up a lot of our lingering questions."

For example, the Prodigies could find out what precisely the evil dragon was. They could determine whether it was safe to ignore it and use Neuro's power to go back to Earth. That enigmatic entity held all the answers the high schoolers sought.

"I've been mentioning a lot of theory and conjecture, and much of what I just said is speculative. However, if it turns out that these rules are literal and not just an allegory, then we can't afford to ignore that Rule 1 implies that the entire planet is in danger. And we're not going to take Neuro up on his offer until we get that all squared away. After all...this world is home to people we care about."

"Tsukasa..."

"I need to find out if it's really all right for us to achieve our goal through the method Neuro suggested, and I believe that getting in contact with the entity from Rule 2 is the best way to do that. I know how scary it must be to have a strange voice come and talk to you out of nowhere, but would you be willing to set that aside and help me?"

If all the Prodigies wanted was to get home no matter what, then it was as simple as asking Neuro for his help. Yet that's not what they had done. Ensuring their friends were safe came first.

And because of that—

"Of course."

—Lyrule had no reason to turn him down.

"I'm curious about who she is, too. And if the woman who spoke to me is the same person who summoned you all into this world, then she might know how to get you back, too."

"Thanks. That means a lot to me."

"Oh, there's no need to thank me... If this evil dragon truly exists, then we need to know about it as soon as possible. And also...I might have been surprised at first, but I don't think the woman behind the voice is a bad person. I don't know *why* I get that feeling, but I do."

"I share the sentiment."

When the entity spoke to Tsukasa through Lyrule, he hadn't sensed any ill will from it. He may have had a few complaints about their turbulent summoning and the way he and the other Prodigies had nearly died when they first arrived here, but compared to Neuro, the enigmatic being had given a much better—

No, that's enough.

Tsukasa ended that particular thought there. He didn't have nearly enough information yet to know whether he could trust Neuro *or* the entity. Rendering judgment now would be jumping to conclusions. After admonishing himself for getting swayed by first impressions, Tsukasa gripped the steering wheel tightly—

"Hmm... Looks like we're coming up on our destination."

—and accelerated toward the towering checkpoint that came into view when they broke through the tree line.

The structure was made of white-lacquered walls and burnt timber. A watchtower sat atop its fortified aperture. This was the entrance that led from the imperial mainland to the Yamato dominion—the Rashomon Gate.

"Wh-what is that thing?!"

"Why's that box moving all on its own?!"

"S-stop right there! Name yourselves!"

Trucks were far beyond anything this world had seen before. Whenever a native saw one, they had pretty much the same reaction. And the imperial soldiers guarding the Rashomon Gate were no exception. They flew into a panic and rushed toward the vehicle with weapons in hand.

Tsukasa got out on his own—

"Lower your weapons. We're the ambassadors from the Republic of Elm. Surely you must have been informed that we'd be meeting the Yamato administrator here, no?"

—and spoke with the utmost calm and composure despite the spearheads leveled at him.

Upon hearing that, the middle-aged *byuma*, who looked to be the captain, recovered from his shock. His back straightened, he ordered his men to stow their arms, and he gave Tsukasa a salute.

"M-my deepest apologies…! I'll call for the administrator at once, so if you wait a moment, you can—"

"Whoa, your carriage is just as freaky as they say."

Midway through the captain's sentence, a glib voice cut him off. When Tsukasa shifted his gaze to see who it was—

"Like, bruh, you forgot your horses (LOL)."

—he saw a dark-skinned *hyuma* emerge from inside the Rashomon Gate and stroll toward the truck. His lips hung in an easygoing grin, while his gaze wandered about listlessly. The gait he carried himself with could only be described as lackadaisical. Simply put, this man conducted himself quite flippantly. However, it was clear from his overcoat and ostentatious adornments that he held a high position in the empire.

Could it be?

As the thought crossed Tsukasa's mind, the captain spoke up in surprise.

"M-Mr. Administrator. Weren't you taking a nap?"

"I *was*, till y'all started yapping up a storm."

After firing off a complaint, the man walked over to Tsukasa and introduced himself in the casual way that he seemed to do everything.

"Hey, hey, hey! The name's Jade von Saint-Germain, and word on the street's that I'm the administrator of the Yamato dominion. Whazzaaaaaap."

It wasn't the politest introduction ever, yet while Ringo and Lyrule had since followed Tsukasa out of the truck, Aoi was still snoozing in the front seat. Thus, Tsukasa was hardly in a position to criticize the other party's conduct. With a smirk, he reached out for a handshake as he introduced his party.

"I'm Tsukasa, the angel of the Seven Luminaries entrusted with matters of state. The two behind me are Ringo, another of the Seven Luminaries' angels, and Lyrule, an ambassador from the Republic of

Elm. The one sleeping in the truck is Aoi, also an angel. We're counting on your guidance to reach the dominion's seat of government, Administrator Jade."

Jade yawned, then replied with apparent disinterest, "Honestly, this is all kind of a pain in the ass, but I guess it's my job, so I gotta... Huh?" The moment the man returned Tsukasa's handshake, he spotted Lyrule and Ringo. His previously listless eyes lit up.

"...Is something the matter?" inquired Tsukasa.

"'Is something the matter?' 'Is something the *matter*?' My dude, my guy, my pal! Your party's packed to the brim with hotties! Has Elm *always* been babeland? See, this is what I'm talkin' about!"

""Uh...""

"Look, when I heard that a bunch of country randos started a rebellion, I figured they'd all be uggos. My motivation levels? Zero across the board. But if you're telling me I get to play host to a buncha bombshells, then count me the hell in! Damn, I'm getting hyped already!"

Jade's attitude had done a complete one-eighty. He strode past Tsukasa and approached the girls.

"Hello, hello, hello! What's a guy gotta do to get your names?"

"..."

"Uh, um, I'm pretty sure...Tsukasa just told you them..."

"Ah yeah, my B. I got this disease thing—when anyone but a cute girl tells me something, it just goes in one ear and out the other. So I'm begging you here, give 'em to me one more time! I'm on my hands and knees!"

"A-all right, all right. I'm Lyrule, representing the Republic of Elm. It's nice to meet you."

"Lyrule! Lychee! Lycchi! Lycchi!"

"L-Lycchi?!"

"What a good-ass name! Whaddaya say, Lycchi? Wanna blow

off the snoozefest negotiation stuff and take the Yamato grand tour instead? Act fast, and the offer comes good with a guide who knows everywhere that's hip and happening in the whole dominion! Girl, I could use both hands, and I still wouldn't have enough fingers to count all the choice watering holes I know, so you *know* I gotchu covered."

"Um, that's… I'm not…"

It was probably the first time in her life that Lyrule had been hit on so aggressively. As she gave him a stiff smile that did little to hide her discomfort, she shot pleading looks at Tsukasa. And as for Ringo, she had already taken refuge behind Lyrule and kept her gaze firmly fixed on the ground.

"We appreciate the kind offer, but I'm afraid we have to decline." Unable to just sit and watch, Tsukasa placed a hand on Jade's shoulder and lightly laid on the pressure to tell him to back off. "As appealing as such recreational activities sound, we have a more pressing matter to attend to—one that we came all the way to Yamato in order to address. I'm sure you can appreciate that, Administrator Jade."

Thankfully, Jade got the message.

"My bad, my bad. Got carried away there."

He took a couple of steps back to give Lyrule her personal space.

"Came on a bit strong for a first impression, huh? Sorry 'bout that. I guess playboy just kinda runs in my blood, but I figured it was my duty as an imperial gentleman to keep the ladies entertained. Feels like I didn't bring the right energy into the room, though… Wait, hold up. Are you and the hotties, like, an item?"

""———!!""

Jade raised his pinkie as he asked, a gesture used in some parts to signal that one was talking about romance.

Lyrule's and Ringo's cheeks went bright red at the crass question.

"C'mon, dude, you gotta tell me this stuff sooner. I've got mad

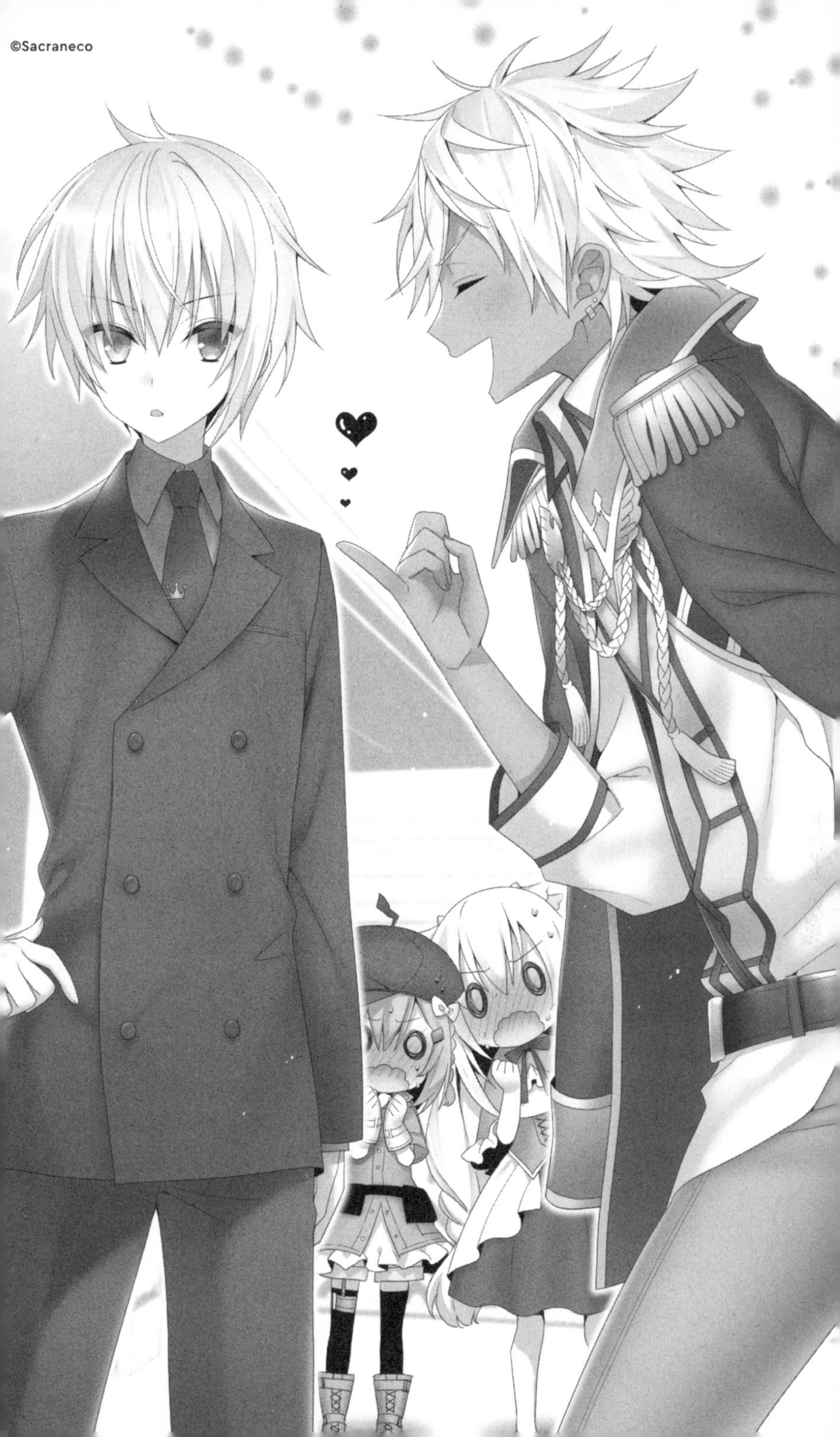

respect for the bro code, but I can be kinda slow on the uptake, y'feel me?"

"The girls and I don't have that kind of relationship. We're just good friends." Tsukasa's reply set Jade straight, informing him that he had misunderstood. However, he didn't stop there. "As their friend, though, and as someone who knows them quite well, I should mention that Ringo and Lyrule don't respond well to that aggressive style of conversation. The way I see it, you left them fairly frazzled. I appreciate how welcoming you're being, but I ask that you take their feelings into account as well."

When it came to telling people off, Tsukasa was nothing if not tactful.

"Gotcha! Consider it done!" Jade replied understandingly.

""*Sigh…*"" Lyrule's and Ringo's shoulders slumped a little as they watched the exchange.

Friends.

They knew that Tsukasa didn't mean any harm by it. Yet both of them harbored feelings a little more passionate than acquaintanceship toward him, so hearing the young man deny Jade's statement so flatly hurt a little. Unfortunately, someone noticed that.

"*Huh? Did you two just get bummed out by that?*" Jade whispered.

""!!!!""

At his inquiry, the girls choked back shrieks and nearly leaped out of their socks. That response was answer enough. Jade gave them a satisfied smile.

"*Ah-haaah. So we're talkin' an unrequited love triangle sorta situation. I gotchu, I gotchu,*" he said softly.

"*Ack! Th-that's not—*," Lyrule quietly tried to deny it, but there was no stopping Jade.

"*Well, my dudettes, you came to the right man! Your guy, uh…what was his name, again? Right, right, Tsukasa. Plan is, while we head to the castle, I'm gonna spend that time thinkin' up some sort of sweet way we can get everyone amped up so y'all can get close to your boy! Make sure you look forward to it, 'cause this party's gonna be off the hook!"*

"I-it's fine! Y-you really don't have to!"

"Don't you worry about a thing! You got me at the helm, and lemme tell you, I can throw a party so litty it'll turn a pair of shy country gals into regular party rockers! I am on this shit! I mean, c'mon, what sorta gentleman goes and abandons a couple of lovestruck girls in need?"

Jade flashed his pearly whites along with a big thumbs-up. Lyrule and Ringo went pale. They needed to stop him. Who knew what mayhem he was about to drag them into?

Unfortunately, fate was not on their side—

"Mr. Administrator, your horse is ready."

"Sweet! All right, Elm gang, follow me!"

—as one of the soldiers chose that moment to bring Jade's steed over and open the Rashomon Gate. It was time to go.

"Plan is: We're makin' a beeline straight for the castle. You sure you're gonna be all right without any horses?"

Jade had seen the truck running earlier, but he asked just to be certain. Tsukasa replied with a nod.

"We'll be fine. In fact, having horses would only slow us down."

"F'real? Damn, that's kinda nuts. Guess that means I'm free to gun it, huh?"

"Be my guest. However…" Tsukasa made his move. "…I do have one request."

"Hit me."

"The most direct route from here to the castle has us passing by three farming villages. I'd like to make a small detour to them."

"What? Why? You tryin' to get some tourism in? There's nothing to see there but rice. And heck, this time of year, the rice hasn't even grown yet."

"I want to examine what sort of conditions your citizens are living in. Princess Kaguya told us that the people of Yamato were in immediate danger. As proponents of equality for all, we have an obligation to at least look into her claims. I hope you don't mind."

...!

Tsukasa was requesting an immediate stop that was not on the original itinerary, and Ringo immediately picked up on what he was after.

If the dominion government was indeed oppressing the people of Yamato as Kaguya claimed, they would have no choice but to deny the appeal. They may have insisted that "*The Yamato dominion government's rule is just and fair, and we would like to demonstrate that fact to you,*" but they had likely only tidied up the places they expected the Elm delegation to observe.

Conversely, if Tsukasa's request went through, it would enable him to glimpse Yamato citizens in their actual environment. No matter how Jade replied, it would provide significant insight into Yamato's current situation. Of course, given what Kaguya had told Tsukasa, the odds of Jade agreeing seemed exceedingly unlikely.

"You got it. We'll end up getting in a bit late, but if you wanna take the scenic route to check out the not-rice, then the scenic route it is."

Huh?

That was how Ringo had gauged the situation, but Jade defied her expectations and readily agreed to Tsukasa's surprise attack.

"...Thank you. Would you mind leading the way?"

"Roger that!!" Jade replied enthusiastically, then took off atop his horse.

In turn, Tsukasa told Ringo and Lyrule to get back in the truck. Ringo did as instructed. As she returned to her seat, she shook her head in puzzlement.

Why did Jade agree to our request so readily?

If Kaguya was right, and the Yamato citizens were in peril, then seeing them go about their days would make that fact painfully clear. The empire wouldn't have time to conceal everything. It would leave them no recourse but to confess to Kaguya's allegations. So why, then?

The question weighed heavy on Ringo's mind. Later, when she saw Yamato for herself, her confusion only deepened.

To make a long story short, when Tsukasa's group dropped by the three farming villages, the problems Kaguya described…were nowhere to be seen. The populace wasn't living like kings, but nothing suggested that they were suffering, either.

Ringo diligently conducted surveys of the settlements' soil and water quality and checked the status of their buildings and infrastructure, but it all appeared adequate. A common problem in situations like theirs was when the colonizers stole all the fertile land from the native people, but that didn't seem to be the case here.

Furthermore, the infrastructure they relied on for their day-to-day lives, such as their bridges, waterwheels, and disaster-prevention facilities like dams, had all undergone regular maintenance. Those spots that had been damaged in the war three years prior had all been repaired.

There was no evidence that the dominion government was neglecting its people. In fact, it would be fair to say that they had it more fairly than those in the former Findolph domain.

Verdant expanses stretched as far as the eye could see, and the sounds of children playing happily echoed in the distance. The sight was downright tranquil. There was no gloom or doom anywhere. And that wasn't just true of the scenery, either. The villagers' hearts were just as unclouded.

"Huh? Destitute? The hell you talkin' about?"

"And for that matter, who are you? Haven't seen you 'round these parts before."

"I mean, sure, we don't live like aristocrats or anything."

"But for us, what we've got here is plenty."

"We got three squares, peaceful lives… What more could we want?"

"Yeah, and it's all thanks to Lady Mayoi hashing out a fair deal with the empire."

"Oh, without a doubt. Lady Mayoi has done so much for us."

"She even opened up trade routes with Freyjagard, and now we've got access to all sorts of new stuff."

"I gotta hand it to the empire. Their bread and their meat ain't half bad. We didn't get many goods from them during Emperor Gekkou's reign, see. Compared to back then, I'd say we're doing pretty good for ourselves."

"Bread's the best!"

While Ringo inspected the infrastructure, Tsukasa canvased the locals, inquiring about their lives and the treatment they were receiving at the hands of the dominion government. However, none he talked to—young and old, men and women alike—had any complaints about the dominion government or expressed any dissent.

It sounded like they held a lot of trust in and gratitude toward the current dominion lord, Princess Mayoi—Kaguya's younger sister and the girl who helped bring Yamato down by aiding the empire in the war.

There was one person they did have some harsh things to say about, however.

"So in other words, the dire straits Princess Kaguya told us about don't exist?" Tsukasa asked.

"Lady Kaguya, huh…"

"I don't know what's going through that head of hers, but I'm no fan of the way she throws baseless accusations around to try to pick a fight with Freyjagard after they've done so right by us."

"Maybe she's jealous of Lady Mayoi or something?"

"I dunno, but I like things nice and peaceful as they are now. If she wants to fight the empire, she should go off and do it on her own."

"You can say that again. That woman needs to control herself."

Not a single person Tsukasa surveyed sympathized with Kaguya and her resistance movement; most seemed to consider her a nuisance.

"…Tsukasa."

After completing her survey of the infrastructure, Ringo called the young man over as he finished jotting down the locals' comments in his notepad.

"Ah, Ringo. What's the verdict?"

"The village…has been properly maintained…just like the last two. Flooding from the rain yesterday…brought down a bridge, but they've already…started repairing it."

"Twenty-four hours, and they've already begun work? Impressive."

"Yeah…" Ringo nodded…then gave Tsukasa a worried look. "Um, Tsukasa… Did Kaguya…say how exactly…they were being oppressed?"

"After our trip here was arranged, I actually asked her about that when I visited her to pick up a *certain something*."

"*No matter what I say, you will not believe me until you witness it for yourself. As such, I would send you into Yamato blind, so you might observe things as they truly are. For when you do, you, too, will realize what hath been wrought,*" Kaguya had stated. And her comment was not without a valid point.

This was an issue that had far-reaching implications on international diplomacy. Tsukasa wasn't about to do something as stupid as taking a single side of the story at face value. Kaguya understood that he would reserve final judgment until he'd seen the situation for himself, and with that being the case, anything she told him might just make him suspicious of her.

If Yamato really was visibly suffering, it didn't make sense to risk earning his distrust when she could simply send him down there to see for himself.

However—

"Are they...really in danger?"

—after seeing Yamato's present state, Ringo couldn't help but harbor doubts.

"There is a possibility that Kaguya was lying to us," Tsukasa replied.

"You...think so?"

"I asked around, and by the sound of it, the Yamato people are more bothered by the resistance movement itself than by anything the dominion government is doing. They think she's damaging their relationship with the empire. In other words, Kaguya and her supporters have failed to earn the trust of the very people they say they're trying to save. And that, in turn, limits their options."

After all, guerrilla warfare only worked when you had support from the locals. The tactics involved required all sorts of resources, from fighters and arms to food and places of operation. Without help from the populace, you would be left with no way to obtain any of those necessities. Thus, Tsukasa had to assume the Yamato resistance forces were in a precarious spot.

"In order to salvage the situation, she might well have twisted and dramatized the truth to fit her narrative in an attempt to get the Seven Luminaries to act. It's not unthinkable."

"..."

Ringo understood what Tsukasa was saying...but she couldn't bring herself to believe it. There was no proof to back up her conviction, but she understood that such a lie would crumble under the slightest scrutiny.

It wouldn't make sense for Kaguya to do something as risky as crash the election announcement and let herself get arrested if all she was armed with was a weak fib. What's more, since the moment Ringo had arrived in Yamato, she hadn't been able to shake the feeling that *something was off.*

Pinpointing it proved challenging, yet when the shy young woman beheld the tranquil, rural landscape and the smiles of its residents… her heart grew uneasy.

As Ringo tried to sort through why she felt that way—

"I must say, though, I'm impressed."

—Tsukasa spoke up from beside her.

"About…what?"

"Despite being left as a mere vassal state of the empire, the dominion government was able to earn the people's trust and rapidly restore their quality of life in a period of fewer than three years. What kind of methods could they have employed to achieve such miraculous results? Strong leadership alone wouldn't have been able to pull this off—they would have needed to work closely with the imperial government as well."

That was quite a political marvel.

"As a fellow politician, I'm interested in finding out what kind of leader orchestrated all this." Tsukasa's voice rang with excitement.

"Yo, you ready to bounce soon? I wanna get to the castle before it gets dark," Jade asked as he approached Tsukasa and Ringo, pressuring them.

Sure enough, the sun was well into its descent.

Yamato's castle was its seat of government, and the dominion lord was expecting them there. It would be rude to keep them waiting any longer on account of Tsukasa's sudden request.

As such—

"Sorry, of course. We'll be all set to go in just a moment."

—Tsukasa agreed readily. He and Ringo made their way back toward the truck where Lyrule and Aoi were waiting.

Suddenly, the villagers began letting out excited cries.

"Hmm?"

They were making such a fuss that Tsukasa, Ringo, and Jade couldn't help but turn their heads to look.

That's when they saw her. There was a young woman about their age dressed in a kimono and riding straight toward them on a horse.

"Hoo boy. Welp, here she comes."

The moment Jade laid eyes on the girl, he let out an exasperated sigh. Atop her steed, she charged straight past Tsukasa and Ringo—

"My booooooo!!"

—then took a flying leap at Jade right out of the saddle.

"Gack!"

Petite as she was, the acceleration she'd built up meant that her body packed a serious wallop. As Jade let out a muffled moan, the young woman laid into him with tears in her eyes.

"You're late! You promised you'd be back by, like, sundown, so what gives? Why're you dillydallying all the way out here?! Oooh, I'm so mad I can't even!"

Her voice was so shrill it caused collateral damage to all within earshot.

Tsukasa and Ringo knitted their brows at the aural assault, but Jade replied with a familiar tone. "Yeah, that's totes my bad. Our guests wanted to take a detour, so I figured I'd be a good host and show 'em some hospitality. Service is my middle name, y'know." He gently set the girl embracing him down on the ground as he apologized.

The girl's pouty expression softened. "Oh, Jade... You're too darn nice; that's your problem. But that's what I love about you."

The pair exchanged a very public kiss.

Ringo and Tsukasa watched it all unfold in blank shock. The former's face flushed red at the girl's bold behavior, but Tsukasa was more distracted by her distinctive physical features—namely, her long ears. They were identical to Lyrule's and Kaguya's.

"Administrator Jade. Is she, by any chance...?"

Jade shrugged and gave Tsukasa a pained smile. "Yeah, basically. The plan was to have you guys officially meet her once we got to the castle, but here we are. C'mon, Mayo-Mayo. These peeps came all the way from Elm to see us, so give 'em a nice greeting, 'kay?"

"What's popping?! I'm Mayoi, top biotch of the Yamato dominion. ☆ But also, like, Jade's bae? I guess? Tee-hee. ☆ Anyhoo, sweet to meetcha. ♪ Like, totes!"

This outrageous young lady before them was Princess Mayoi, lord of the dominion and architect behind war-torn Yamato's three years' worth of restoration projects.

It was the same day that Tsukasa and the others left for the discussion in Yamato.

Once it was clear that the Elm national elections would be a battle between the Principles Party and the Reform Party, each side began publicly announcing their policies.

The Reform Party emphasized their relationship with the empire, and the measures they proposed were designed with a peaceful, amiable eye toward international relations.

In contrast, the Principles Party was ready to fight for the sake of equality for all, and they championed the necessity of a large-scale expansion of armaments and patriotic arrangements to help the people realize the pride they held as the world's moral vanguards.

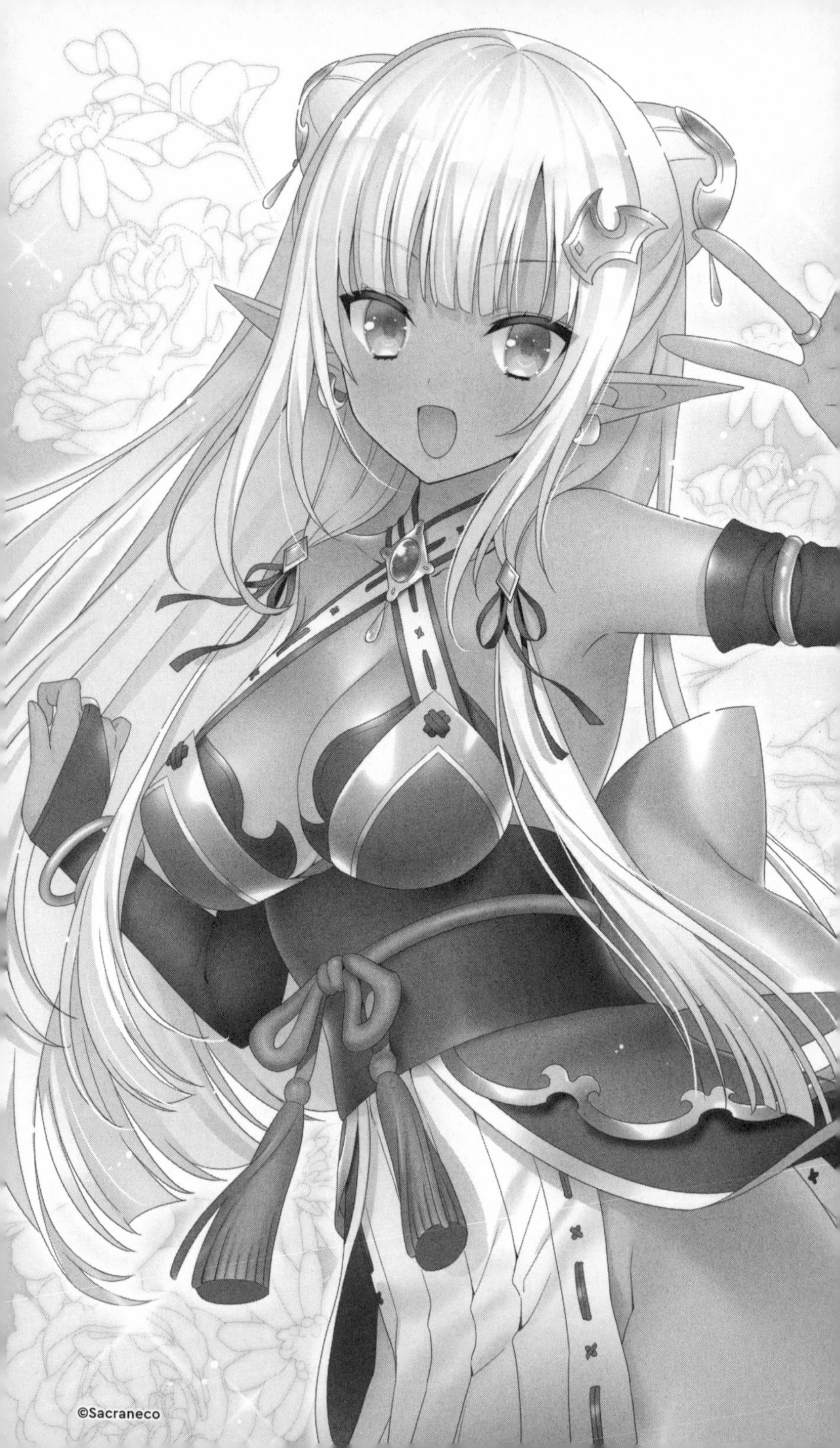
©Sacraneco

With Juno and Tetra commanding their respective groups, the two forces heatedly debated their stances all across Elm.

Each faction was utterly convinced that theirs was the side of justice. And they both saw themselves as people fit to guide the path of a nation.

That fact alone marked a significant victory for the People's Revolution that the Prodigies started.

Unfortunately, a dark presence was budding in the shadow of their radiant zeal.

It was precisely the *malice that followed in democracy's wake* that Tsukasa had mentioned in his conversation with Shinobu.

"Long live democracy."

In the evening, while Tsukasa and Ringo met Mayoi over in Yamato, a man cloaked in a long robe approached a manor in the Gustav province. He stopped before the doorman and praised democracy. The doorman responded with a nod and opened the door.

Those words were the passphrase.

The man hurried inside, then jogged down the hallway. From there, he opened the door at the end of the corridor and entered.

In it, a group of dignified gentlemen was seated around a large round table with the light of dusk streaming down on them. One, an older, tough-looking bald man, spoke to the robed newcomer.

"Good work, Comrade Donitz. I trust it all went as planned?"

The man doffed his robe, revealing the gaunt face of the thirtysomething beneath it. His name was Morgan Donitz, and he was a Principles Party candidate running in the Archride domain who worked as an accountant for a local company.

Donitz replied with a spring in his step and excitement in his voice. "It did! Archride and Buchwald used to be in the Reformists' pocket, but support is slowly shifting to the Principles Party! It went exactly like you said it would, Glaux!"

The announcement elicited cheers from the gentlemen around the table. As it turned out, it wasn't just Donitz. Every person sitting there was a Principles Party candidate running in one of the many elections across Elm.

The bald old man from before narrowed his eyes with a grandfatherly look on his face. His plump white mustache quivered as he laughed. "Hoh-hoh-hoh. I told you, didn't I? If you're going to run, do it with the Principlists."

"Yeah, you did. But how'd you know the Principles Party would end up on top?"

"Because nobody wants to treat someone they think they're superior to as an equal," Glaux explained.

After winning their independence from Freyjagard in an overwhelming fashion, the people of Elm had grown conceited and began thinking of themselves as better and more enlightened than the imperials. Many of them, the youth demographic in particular, thought it was ridiculous to consider the empire's whims at all.

"Simply spouting off patriotic drivel gives them delusions of valor and grandeur more intoxicating than the strongest opium."

Everyone would rather be a hero than a coward. Glaux knew that when it came to matters of publicly debating their platforms and philosophies, the Principles Party's appeals to bravery and patriotism would naturally give them an edge. The gentlemen around the table applauded Glaux's prescience.

However—

"B-but, Glaux... Are you sure it's all right for us to be making such extreme guarantees about liberating Yamato and starting a holy war if Freyjagard resists? The Seven Luminaries gave us mighty weapons, but if the emperor's main forces come back from abroad, won't we just get crushed by their sheer numbers?"

—one of them expressed some doubts.

The campaign promises they were making to rile up would-be heroes were dangerous. Fulfilling them meant risking their lives. However, Glaux just scoffed at the dissenter's concerns.

"Hoh-hoh-hoh. As if we would actually make good on those pledges."

"What…?! The people will never forgive us…!"

Behind Glaux's pleasant, grandfatherly smile, his eyes gleamed like a raptor's as he spoke to the bewildered man.

"So? Why should we need their forgiveness?"

"Huh?"

"Campaign promises are just empty words meant to sway over fools—nothing more, nothing less.

"Once you win an election, you remain in power until the next election rolls around three years later.

"That means that for that entire period, it doesn't matter if we honor our word or not. Either way, we'll be protected by the fact that we were 'chosen by the people.' As long as we possess that shield, we're free to drain Elm dry. Besides, even if war did happen to break out…it would be little more than an annoyance. Think about it. *We* wouldn't be the ones doing the dying."

"_____!"

"No, that would be the pawns we send to the front lines. Our only task would be to move them about from the safety of the rearguard while sipping wine as we are now. Should the rabble start to demand someone's head on a stake…we can serve that stupid woman up to them."

Stupid woman.

Hearing the phrase brought sadistic smiles to the gentlemen's lips. The one in question was none other than Tetra.

She may have been the Principles Party's leader, but the men who employed the party to mask their true intentions thought of her as little more than a jester.

The sympathy she felt for the plight of Yamato and her desire to rescue them just as she had been were genuine. Yet as these men saw it, there were far better ways to use political power.

Embezzling funds. Receiving kickbacks. Writing legislation to make their corruption go more smoothly. The list went on and on.

"The election will be moving into its final stage soon. And word is that Tsukasa, the angel who's been running the interim government, has gone off to Yamato. We need to strike while the iron is hot. It's time to move the *plan* into immediate effect. By stirring up a wave of anti-imperial sentiment, we'll drive the masses toward nationalist beliefs. With that, our victory will be unassailable.

"Hoh-hoh-hoh. Who could have dreamed that winning a few idiots over with platitudes would let us shape the nation and its laws to our will without having to expose ourselves to a shred of danger? I've never seen a more profitable business venture in my life. We owe the Seven Luminaries' angels a great debt for making politics accessible to those like us."

"You can say that again."

"Yeah, for sure."

"The future's looking bright, gents! I'll drink to that!"

"Long live democracy!"

"Hear, hear!"

"Hear, hear!"

The conspirators clinked their wine glasses together. Every face in the room bore a sickening smirk plastered across it. Although it was a gathering of people who might soon be responsible for leading the Republic of Elm, there was no concern for the future to be found there—only degeneracy and corruption.

It was precisely what Tsukasa had been worried about. One of the darker aspects of democracy was that anyone could get involved, no matter how incompetent or wicked they were. People would come out of the woodwork who had no pride, no ideals, and no sense of responsibility.

These types were only concerned with how a country's power could be manipulated to line their pockets. These people were no statesmen—merely vultures.

AFTERWORD

Thank you all for buying and reading *High School Prodigies*, Vol. 5.

Between all the things I have to keep track of, all the foreshadowing there is to juggle, and how generally hard the series is to write, its *Choyoyu* (Prodigiously Easy) nickname is really starting to get to me. This has been Riku Misora, self-destructing.

Sorry about the long delay between the last volume and this one.

In case you didn't know, the Panjandrum that showed up this time around is a weapon that truly existed. Wow. Just, wow. You had a country put all the best and brightest in a room together during a war, and that's what they came up with? What were they *putting* in that tea?

However, as hard as I was on the Panjandrum in the story, there's an interesting theory that its development was actually an advanced misinformation tactic to trick Nazi Germany into defending the wrong front and leaving Normandy vulnerable.

If that's true, then it turns out that the Panjandrum wasn't a failure at all, but a fantastic weapon that played a crucial role in helping the Allies emerge victoriously.

So while it seems useless at first, maybe it's secretly really awesome. And if you ask me, that's pretty cool.

For my money, though, it doesn't get any sweeter than the railway gun. Railway guns are like a more modern version of Mons Meg, the cannon briefly mentioned in the narrative.

Despite having access to cutting-edge technology, Nazi Germany used it to re-create the same weapon that had failed all those centuries ago. It didn't make any sense.

While it might not have amounted to much, you have to admit that it looked slick, and on paper, it was as badass as could be. It was like every little boy's dream made real. And I'm clearly not the only one who feels that way, because many works of fiction pay homage to the Mons Meg.

I think the first time I saw it was when I saw *Arc the Lad*. I was totally blown away by how cool it looked and how awesome an idea it was.

Mayonnaise got to display its fearsome power yet again. Believe me when I say that mayonnaise and salmon really do go amazingly together.

I'll admit that putting mayonnaise on salted fish isn't great for you when it comes to your sodium intake, but I still can't stop myself from spreading it all over my lightly salted autumn salmon.

Now, there are some who say that the mayo ruins the meat by overwhelming its flavor, but I assert that they're wrong. The fatty sourness of the mayonnaise doesn't *overwhelm* the salmon's flavor; it *accentuates* it. After all, you don't get that same taste by just eating mayonnaise straight, now, do you? It's a match made in heaven.

As it happens, in the Misora household, we practice the forbidden art of mixing yuzu paste in with our mayonnaise. We'd already tried plain mayo and wasabi mayo with our dried squid, so we figured that yuzu paste might be good, too, and sure enough, when we tried it, it was delicious. If anybody reading this likes a little kick with their salt, I highly recommend giving it a shot.

The sodium contents are through the roof, though, so make sure you practice moderation. Otherwise, your kidneys will fail at Mach speed.

As you know, this story ended by showing the evil that no democracy can avoid—the "vultures" who want to use politics as a business for personal gain. Even with Tsukasa and the others having gone to Yamato, things will be heating up back in Elm as well.

I plan to demonstrate the ugly parts of democracy as well as its good sides. So the next book is probably going to be the most tumultuous, jam-packed installment yet... Honestly, I'm a bit worried about the page count. I hope it doesn't end up as gigantic as Volume 4, buuuut...

Finally, I'd like to express my gratitude toward the people who helped make this book a reality.

First off, to my editor, Kohara: Once again, thank you for walking across this tightrope with me. And to Sacraneco as well, thank you for the consistently wonderful illustrations. I doubt I could have made the June release date without you two.

Next, I'd like to thank Kotaro Yamada for working on the manga adaptation that's running in *Young Gangan* and *Gangan GA*. I always look forward to getting my copies!

At the time of writing this, the manga version is in the middle of Volume 2's story line. It's only just started touching on the darkness lurking in the Gustav domain, but seeing the inn-slash-butcher's-den come to life in the manga was downright hair-raising.

It's obviously a bit late now, but it makes me wish I'd included even more horror elements.

Finally, I'd like to express my heartfelt appreciation to everyone who purchased Volume 5. Thank you for buying it after I kept you waiting for so long. It's all because of you that my works keep getting published. I fear I'm starting to repeat myself now, but again, thank you.

I think that's about it for this one. I hope we meet again in the next afterword, but for now, I bid you adieu.

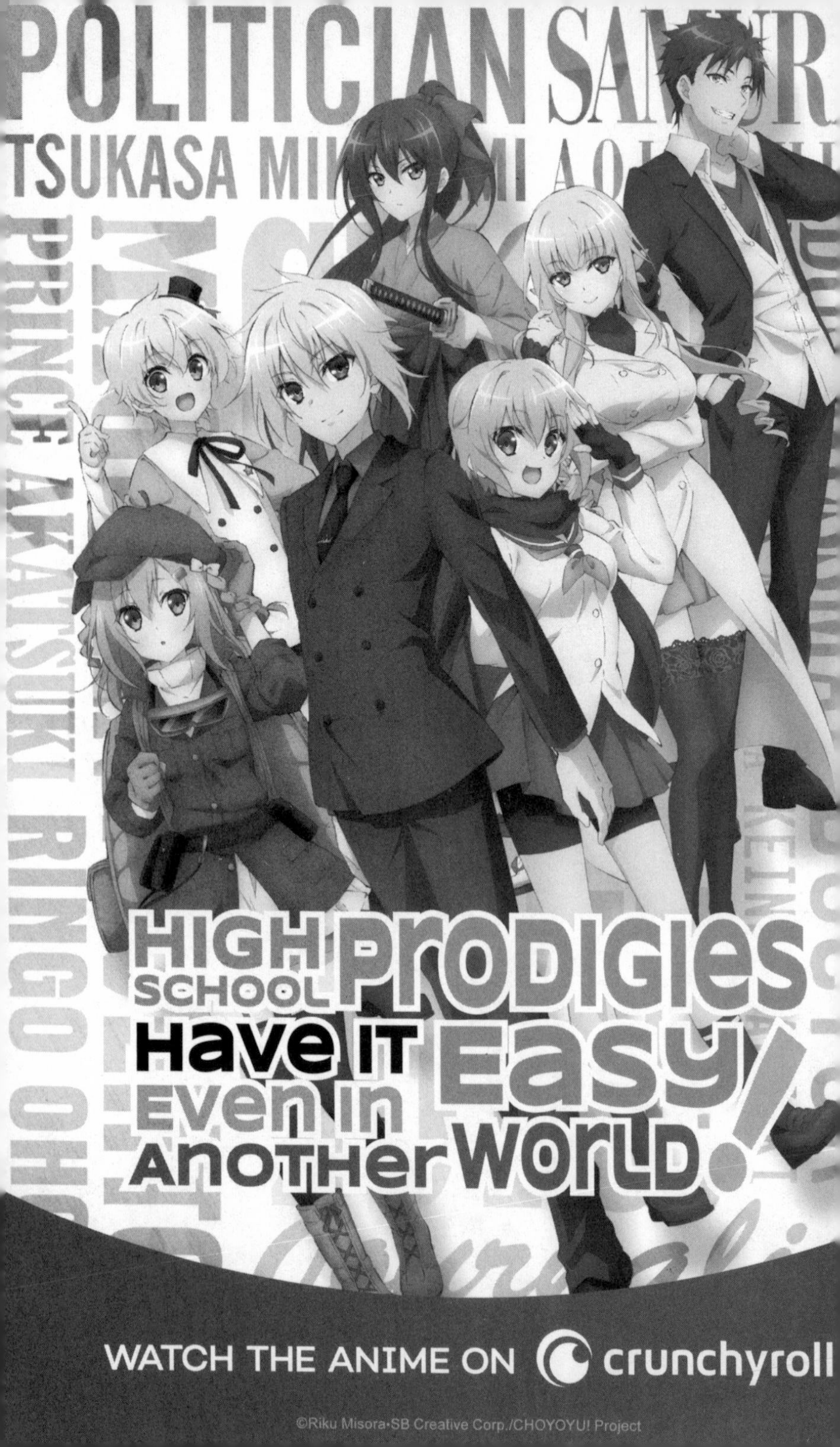
HIGH SCHOOL PRODIGIES HAVE IT EASY EVEN IN ANOTHER WORLD!
WATCH THE ANIME ON crunchyroll
©Riku Misora•SB Creative Corp./CHOYOYU! Project